Tepper's keen eye and darkly dry humor make for a restless yet precise chronicle. By all means, get in this rain-soaked taxi, walk into the shadows, follow the sound of doors slammed, because Susan Tepper's "*What Drives Men*" is going to challenge your notions of strength, loyalty, and love.

– Michael Dwayne Smith, Editor/Publisher of *Mojave River Press & Review*

Susan Tepper's *What Drives Men* is a picaresque masterpiece. Tepper's cast of characters: a Gulf War vet, an octogenarian C&W singer, and three twenty-three year-olds, are as diverse a group of nutcases you'll come across this side of The Master and Margarita. Tepper spins a marvelous tale, sure to tickle the funny bone.

– James Claffey, author of *The Heart Crossways* and *Blood A Cold Blue*

What Drives Men is a different kind of road novel, as Russell is a different kind of journey-man. Fun, odd, engaging, and even moving, you can't anticipate where you're going or when you'll get there. It's a delightful ride though, as much a trip for the reader as it is for Russell. As with him, things will move you off where you've gotten stuck, and get you going to where you really need to be. I enjoyed the ride immensely.

– David S. Atkinson, author of *The Garden of Good and Evil Pancakes* and *Bones Buried in the Dirt*

WHAT DRIVES MEN

First Edition
ISBN 978-1-73311-850-7

Wilderness House Press
145 Foster Street
Littleton MA 01460

www.wildernesshousepress.com

Wilderness House Literary Review
www.whlreview.com

Book designed by Steve Glines
Text: Gandhi Serif

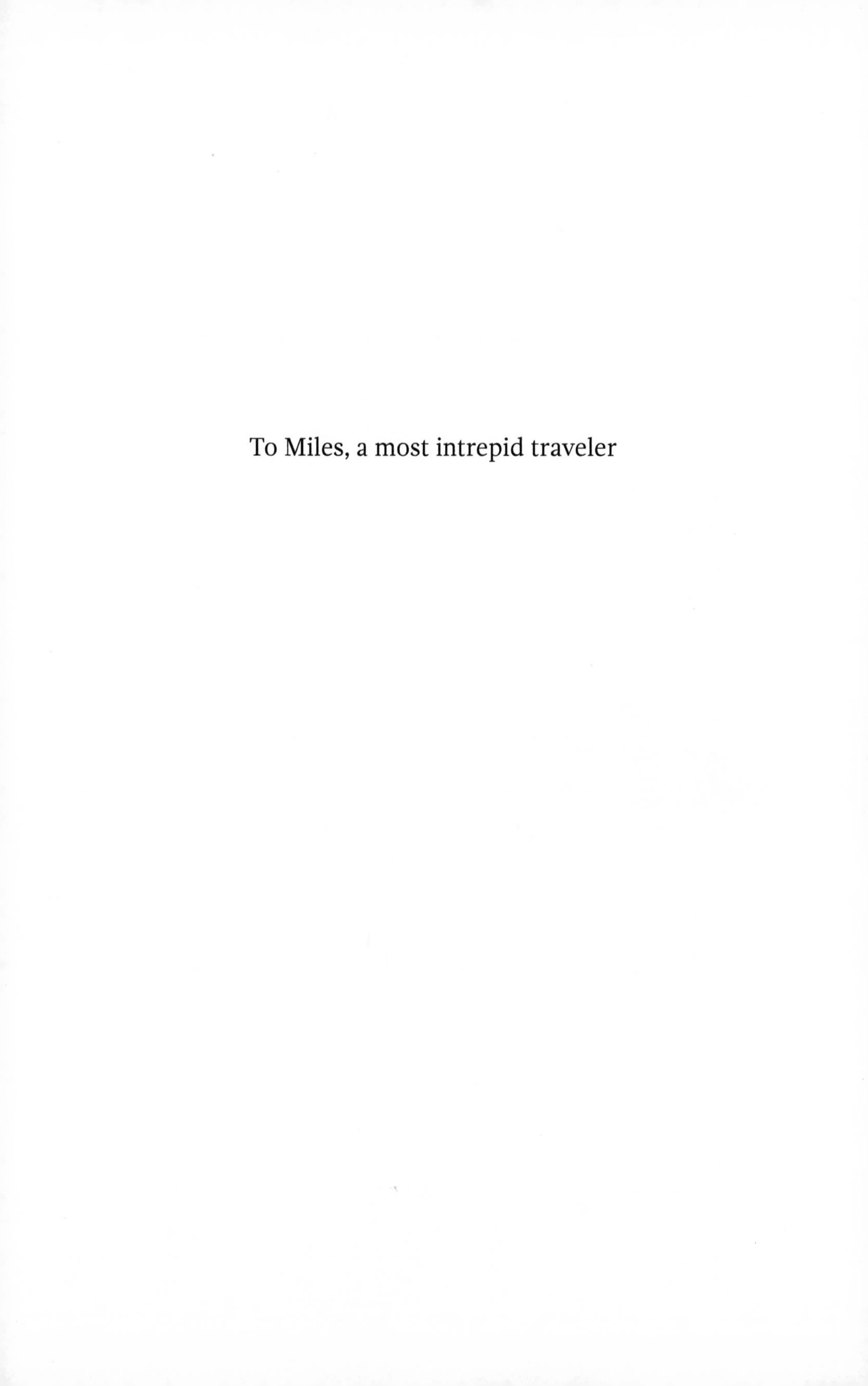

To Miles, a most intrepid traveler

OTHER BOOKS BY SUSAN TEPPER

Monte Carlo Days & Nights
dear Petrov
The Merrill Diaries
From the Umberplatzen
What May Have Been
Deer & Other Stories
Blue Edge

"This is the house where I say goodbye."
— Hermann Hesse

"Nothing changes except what has to."
— Captain Donald Cragen, Law & Order

WHAT DRIVES MEN

A Novel

Susan Tepper

Wilderness House Press

PROLOGUE

Should I come with you he thought of asking then knew it would sound idiotic. Maggie. Magpie. Good ole Mags. Marching room to room shoving clothes and other things in suitcases. He watched her put her address book and little tin recipe box into an already jammed bag; kneeling on its canvas side in order to get it zipped. Maggie was strong – he had to give her that. Russell followed behind, room by room, refusing to help. Why should he? None of it was his idea. Not that she'd asked for help. Not her. When she was done, bags zipped, coat on, she phoned for a taxi. Dark-blue suitcases like sentries standing guard in the kitchen. Russell stood in the hall, just past the archway. They waited it out in silence. When the taxi finally got there its horn blared. Russell stepped further back into the shadows. Let her leave all alone, he thought. Let her wonder what will become of me. He heard the back door slam. Went to the living room and sat on the sofa. He heard the taxi start up then pull away, down the long hill of their driveway. He could feel the taxi driver's foot on the brake pedal all the way down to the road. *Hesitation* he thought; hoping. The taxi noise fainter and fainter. After that Russell felt nothing.

CHAPTER 1

Raging

Playful he was thinking a moment earlier, watching the squirrel scramble up the trunk of a big oak. Fall had come early and they were charging everywhere. A lot of his backyard torn up from their buried nuts.

Part way up the tree it must've decided to make an about-face, throwing itself squarely onto his neck. *I'm going to die* had crashed through Russell's mind as the squirrel dug deep into his throat.

After he passed out, then came to, he was unable to offer any specific information. Some people had gathered around. A few women with baby strollers and a police officer. The women presumably from this neighborhood. On his back in the street Russell couldn't recall having seen them before. Two blonds. A third woman who looked darkly foreign. He thought he smelled a type of oil or perhaps even incense coming off her. Russell inhaled. Then her odor seemed taken by the breeze (cool-ish with an underlying warmth was how he would later describe that day).

The police officer, pad and pen poised for writing, stared down at him. He thought the officer looked young.

As for the sky – as viewed beyond dappled leaves not yet fallen from that tree; that particular tree; thereafter to be known by Russell as *the squirrel tree* – the sky that day just happened to be a pure raging blue.

"It bit me," he said. "It jumped out of that tree and it bit me."

The women murmured. The young police officer cleared his throat. "Sir, there is no blood."

"What!"

He tried sitting up but the officer pressed him back down.

"Don't try and move," he told Russell.

"Well if there's no blood... I don't understand. I felt it sink its teeth in my neck."

"Maybe it was the claws," said one of the women.

"Even if it was the claws you'd still have blood," said another.

"Blood, claws, what's the difference!" This third voice less flat than the others who sounded like they ironed their vocal cords.

Russell couldn't stand that dry, offhand way these younger generation women spoke. As if some emotion, a little *feeling* in their tone, might somehow jeopardize their position in the world. Though what that might be, he had no idea.

"With the rising real estate market this has become a dangerous neighborhood!" said the perkier voice.

Dangerous! Russell tried sitting up again only to be shoved down. "Did you check for gunshot wounds?"

"Ladies step away!" barked the police officer.

"Law enforcement in this town is practically non-existent." This from the flat voice Russell recognized as suggesting the claws.

"Yeah, the cops did *zilch* when my xenon headlights were stolen right off my driveway," said another one.

"OK, Ladies! There'll be no more chat." The police officer frowning down on *him*! "Not another word until the ambulance gets here."

Ambulance! Russell felt himself growing chilled, though it had been a nice enough day when he started his walk into town – close to sixty would be his guess, if he were a betting man. Not to mention all that sunshine pouring down. Underneath him, the blacktop surface felt cold, almost slimy. Crushed gravel set into wet tar then rolled. *Messy* he was thinking, bits of loose gravel sticking to his palms. All summer his mother had been warning him. *Trouble ahead* the old woman kept saying. Russell assumed she was turning senile. And that gypsy woman, too – always waving the red flag – that Clara. The one his brother Stan dated up through Labor Day. She had mentioned some kind of trouble. Naturally Russell paid no attention.

"I'm all alone in the world," he said when the police officer asked about his next of kin.

The women murmured again. Pleasantly harmonic, he thought; somewhat surprised. He shifted on his back favoring his left side, certain the sweetest voice must belong to the darkly foreign one he'd glimpsed briefly – naming her *Fig. Sweet Fig.* Though he'd barely seen her, that didn't stop him picturing her breasts, ripe, with their dark nipples.

"I wonder if it's carrying rabies," said the flat voice.

Russell stiffened clutching his neck.

"Sir, I wouldn't do that if I were you. You don't want to touch the wound."

"You said there isn't any blood!"

"True enough. Still it's best to be careful with these things. No point risking infection."

The young officer had a frank expression, innocent-seeming. Innocent of the worst sorts of things policemen see regularly. "How old are you, Son?" he asked the police officer.

In December Russell would turn fifty.

The officer bristled swiping at his nose with the back of his hand. "I won't have that kind of talk."

Russell sighed. OK, he thought. OK.

Staring up into *the squirrel tree* he wondered what had become of it? Small, gray, furry. Gray, he thought again. Enigmatic. Squirrels everywhere. Dashing across roofs, along gutters and fences. The neighborhood overflowing.

"Sir, I'm going to have to frisk you," the officer said.

"What!"

"Just lie still and it'll be over in a moment." He knelt on the ground patting Russell down.

"But I don't have a weapon!"

The officer stood. "Sir, I can see that all is A-OK."

A-OK? Russell stared up at him. Has the whole world gone mad?

When the ambulance finally got there, and the ambulance workers each took a turn looking at his neck, they told Russell he could go home. "Stay there," said the burly-looking guy. "Stay inside. And for Pete's sake lock your door."

Everyone laughed. Everyone, that is, except Russell. By then he was on his feet – the skinnier ambulance guy having given him the nod. He glanced over at the women then brushed off the seat of his pants. "Thank god," he said.

From one of the strollers a baby began squalling. *Sweet Fig* turned out deeply disappointing. Instead of earthy, she was more the short squat type. On equal ground with them now, he decided Sweet Fig did not sound remotely foreign but more from the borough of Queens. In the baggy brown sweatshirt she looked bulky. Then he contemplated the sex of the squirrel that ripped him. He'd seen some covert ops go down in Desert Storm. Turning the possibilities over in his mind. Squirrel, he decided.

"It attacked me for no good reason," Russell said.

"Go home and sleep it off." And the young police officer gave him a light, friendly swat on the back.

The women laughed again. That started the ambulance guys going, everyone getting their rocks off at his expense.

"Fine," said Russell. "Fine. I've seen a few things myself. In The Gulf."

"Shrimp?" said the bulky guy.

"No, The Gulf War." He paused, waiting. Something. Anything. Nobody uttered a word. Then he caught some movement high in the tree – quick, darting, and *poof* it was gone.

CHAPTER 2

No Sure Way

By some miracle he made it home, pausing at the bottom of the driveway, staring up the steep incline shaded by mature maples and a neighbor's giant Norwegian Spruce. Havens. For all sorts of terror. What choice did he have? He couldn't use the thirteen concrete steps leading to his front door since broken hinges barely held the door in its frame. His standard line to anyone unfamiliar with his set up was: *Come 'round back.*

His palms were drenched, he wiped them on his pants. Then pushing Sweet Fig and the others from his mind (though the squirrel couldn't be budged) he started up the driveway – sensing it in there – *pulsing pulsing* – like it entered through his neck and lodged in his skull. His heart was actually banging. *Heart attack*? Sweating was a symptom; he'd heard that. "Just my luck," said Russell. Survive the war and the squirrel, only to drop dead of a heart attack. Felled like a tree, broken, finished; right on his own driveway.

Before she walked out forever, Maggie said he had a failed heart.

What a terrible night. He'd practically jumped down her throat screaming, "Failed heart! What's that? Like a failed grade? Like I failed a course in school?"

Maggie, packing to leave, saying nothing – like he already didn't exist.

❧

Russell made it up the driveway, his back door key jamming in the lock. Wrestling with it, he finally got inside, going straight to the small, blue powder room off the kitchen, switching on the light. Squinting into the mirror. A yellow *Bug Lite* screwed above the medicine cabinet made clear visibility of his wound difficult. How a *Bug Lite* got there... Maggie! He screwed up his face straining toward the mirror – a *Bug Lite* – that would be right up her alley. Afraid of mosquitoes getting trapped in the powder room.

Russell growled. "Bite her ass."

The yellow glare making it virtually impossible to get a clear view of his wound. He barred his teeth, straining to see. Those women today. That gaggle of geese. Nothing to do but stand around watching a man stuck helpless on the ground. Get attacked and women come out of the bushes. Out of nowhere! Since Maggie left, Russell hadn't been able to find any women. Basically, just that crazy Clara-gypsy, and a few of her equally crazy girlfriends his brother Stan carted over as blind dates.

All of a sudden women are crowding around him. Well – not exactly crowding. Though he *had* caught their attention. Seeing him vulnerable like that, they naturally felt obliged to stick around. *Unlike some other people*, he thought, sniffing and going to the living room where he sat down heavily on the sofa, the plastic slip covers letting out a *whoosh*. He took the same middle cushion in the line of three where he sat the night Maggie left.

"Pal," he said patting the sofa, "we're joined at the hip."

Once during their marriage Maggie shoved a whoopee cushion under him. Whether or not he laughed, he can't remember. He wasn't laughing now. But wondering why he chose *here* to sit, not at one side or the other, where at least he'd have an arm rest. He flapped his arms loosely, pondered the squirrel. How it was just doing its thing; then seemed to have a change of heart.

CHAPTER 3

Fluctive

By the next day the temperature had dropped thirty degrees. Everyone on TV who talked weather agreed: It was unusually *fluctive.*

When Russell looked up *fluctive* in his giant WEBSTER – so big and heavy it rested on its own special oak stand in a corner of the dining room – flipping the giant pages he did not find *fluctive.* It should have come between *flub* and *fluctuate.* That oak stand that Maggie bought – her pulpit. He pictured her in a purple robe dispensing advice. To him. She had redecorated the entire house in old oak. Dreary. Feeling disturbed, Russell scratched his head leaving the dining room.

Also disturbing him were thoughts of leaving the house. He'd have to go out soon. His habit of daily food shopping – the fresh meats and fruits and vegetables, the occasional fish or seafood, the bread, bought every day to insure freshness. He was practically out of food. For dinner last night he finished the box of brown rice which he sprinkled with golden raisins to add bulk. The milk was gone and so were the eggs. A little Fontina still clung to the rind, he took it from the refrigerator, scraped it against his top teeth. Then grabbing the phone he called his brother at work. "Stan, I need to talk to Clara can you give me her number?"

His brother made a jerky-sounding laugh. "She won't go out with you, she's got you pegged a-hole for letting Maggie get away so easy. Besides..."

Easy! Nothing about Maggie had ever been easy. He waited for Stan to finish but his brother had gone mute. *Easy* for Stan to say. His wife Tilda died. Fast and clean. One day keeling over at the sink.

Russell rapped a spoon against the countertop. "Besides what?"

"Clara doesn't respect you for staying on disability. That war's been over a looong time."

What business is it of hers? He looked down at his arm; the one clutching the spoon. Short arms. He'd been born that way. Arms, that when fully extended, barely reached his hips. Russell flinched. Little squirrel arms.

"Look, I don't want to date Clara, I want her to give me a reading. That gypsy stuff she does with the cards."

Catching his reflection in the microwave he decided everything about himself could be summed up in one word: tan. Not suntan-tan; nothing that exotic. Just slightly darker than beige.

"My disability is my own business," he said.

"Gulf War's been over a long time, bro."

Russell gritted his teeth. "Desert Storm."

People assumed it was the rifle gave him trouble. The rifle had been a piece of cake, Russell naturally suited to the M-16, his stubby arms becoming an extension of his weapon. It was the climbing got him fucked. He couldn't hold on. The roads were sinkholes. Climbing up top a moving transport vehicle he'd fallen off, breaking his nose and most of the small bones in his face.

"Look, Stan, things have been weird for me lately. Like Clara said they would. She told me some things at the barbecue." He could hear chuckling into the phone.

"Clara *is* good."

"Yeah."

With a little more coaxing Russell got her number. She picked up quickly, her *hello* all summery, musical-sounding. Or was it those birds he could hear in the background? Those tweety birds.

"It's Russell," he announced after making her say hello more than once.

"I've been waiting for you."

"Really?"

They made an arrangement. She would come to him provided he pay twice her normal rate.

"If you can stop by the market and pick up a few things," he added. Reciting his shopping list. Some sparring back and forth. Then both agreeing on four o'clock.

CHAPTER 4

Eggs

Sometime after four-thirty he heard banging on his front door. "Ah, jeez." Russell ambling toward it, looking out a large, diamond-shaped pane then gesturing palms up – a kind of shrug and shouting through the door: "I can't open this, you see, you'll have to *come 'round back*."

She had on a floppy black hat that looked like a car rolled over it. Her face, through the glass, turning red and annoyed. Red as the crushed-velvet cape that spilled from her shoulders. Clara held firm on his stoop, unmoving. A shopping bag of groceries dangling from each hand.

"Russell open up!"

He laughed sheepishly, shrugging again, trying to explain through the door about the hinges; then he laughed once more as if to say *what can I do*?

"Eggs!" She let go of both bags at the same time.

"Oh, god, please, no Clara."

Gingerly opening the door, Russell expecting the worst. She pushed past him going into the house muttering, "Bullshit."

He went outside and picked the bags off the steps. Shutting the front door as carefully as possible, saying to no one in particular, "This door has problems."

In the kitchen he began putting things away, wiggling each egg in the carton to see that none had cracked.

"Let's get going!" she yelled.

He continued to check for breakage.

"Quit fucking with the eggs, Russell."

"How did you know?"

"My cards are getting cold."

CHAPTER 5

Cards

The hat off and tossed aside, her messy brown hair wasn't much of an improvement, though Clara, herself, was neatly arranged: the red velvet cape loosened at the neck and spread around her on the sofa. Russell rubbed his jaw. How dare Stan chastise him! A moment later wondering *was Clara any good in bed*? Stan had never said either way.

Covertly, he continued looking her over. She had on something black and tight under the cape – leggings maybe; maybe a leotard. She took up that same middle cushion where he sat after the squirrel attack; after Maggie left. Pointing he said, "That's a dangerous spot."

"Only if you don't know what you're doing."

She pointed back – a black fingernail wiggling at the chair opposite her. The Tarot deck in a neat pile on the stained glass coffee table. Clara lowering her head to the cards. "Sit down Russell."

He tried cracking a joke. "Those are some *gigunda* cards."

"They're *French* Tarot Cards."

He whistled low through his teeth.

She reached for the cards, the red cape crushing around her like a lot of blood. My blood, thought Russell touching his neck. My missing blood, that is.

"Will you please sit down."

He lowered himself into the chair.

"Do your close friends call you Rusty?"

"I have no close friends."

She raised an eyebrow.

"Well why'd you ask, Clara?"

"It's just one of those things."

"You don't have to be cruel, I've had a terrible time lately. More than lately." He covered his mouth to cough. "A while."

"Of your own doing. Here, shuffle."

"Are you going to explain these cards to me?"

"Cut them in the direction of your heart."

He blinked. His heart. Maggie made that crack – about his heart being a failed heart.

"Like this?" He cut, fumbled the shuffling, a few dropping onto the rug.

She gestured impatiently. "OK, OK, hand them back."

"Aren't you going to tell me what they mean?"

She was turning them over, one by one, across the coffee table.

"No, Russell. No I'm not. That's your trouble. You want answers, all the time, answers." She stared at the cards, her mouth jammed in a tight line.

This troubled him. Her refusal to explain. After all, he was paying. He had a right to know. "What's the point if you're not gonna tell me anything?"

"You got your food didn't you?" She seemed to be focused on a particular card.

What's the matter now? he thought. He coughed again looking away, toward his fish tank – mainly guppies. He should have asked her to pick up fish food. The expensive tropical fish were mostly gone, having met their end around the time he met his end with Maggie. He tried smiling. "I *am* paying you, Clara."

She shook her head, the long silver earrings jangling. "You got the cheap rate." She stifled a yawn. "Being that I know your brother and all. Stan."

"Yes I know his name."

She peeled off more cards till they made a kind of strange but interesting pattern across the stained glass. Almost blinding, thought Russell. Crazy cards on colored glass. Beyond his reach or understanding. It started to give him a headache but Clara seemed fine. She seemed to perk up. While Russell felt a bleakness settle over, similar to a stretch of bad weather.

She leaned back into the sofa and crossed her legs. "In this world you get what you pay for."

"Yesterday I got attacked by a squirrel. I think it was a squirrel. How do you explain that?"

"Was it an American squirrel?"

"How should I know?"

"What kind of tail did it have? Did it have a typical bushy squirrel tail or was it a long skinny tail, kind of sick looking? Like it got chewed off by some other rodent."

He gripped the chair arms. *Rodent* she said. He guessed it was. Still. Rodents he'd always associated with mice, or rats, spreading fear and disease. Plagues, even.

"Didn't the bubonic plague start from rats?" Clara didn't answer. He couldn't answer about the squirrel tail.

"Well? Well? Well?" One of her needle sharp shoes tapped the edge of the coffee table. "What kind of tail?"

Stalling, Russell gazed around the living room, focusing on the barometer – a gift from his mother. Possibly a wedding gift. He couldn't remember. Stuck on *SNOW* all these years, technically it was useless.

"How does a barometer get broken? Could you at least tell me that much, Clara?"

Pursing her lips she plucked something off her knee, examining what looked like a white thread. "That particular barometer?" She stifled a yawn. "I don't know."

"I hope I'm not boring you, Clara."

"Look – you have to take pleasure where you can find it."

What? What's she belching up now? "I take no pleasure in a broken barometer. If that's what you mean."

She rested her head back against the sofa. "You must've dropped it. Knocked it off course."

"Does it have a course?"

"Everything has a course. God, you make me tired! What color was that squirrel anyway? Gray or black?"

"Whoever heard of a black squirrel?"

"Look – there's black ones and there's gray ones." Her voice sounding thin like the oxygen had been siphoned off. "I'm sorry I ever came here." She sat up straight and rubbed her eyes.

"Why did you come here?"

"You seemed desperate. A real desperado." She made a laugh like rattling bones.

Russell stood up, clenching and unclenching his toes.

"You should watch the anger," she said. "The anger's gonna do you in."

He stood staring at her.

"OK. So I guess it's your sneakers are too tight." She laughed again, shrugging. "You do squeeze your ass a lot. I noticed at Stan's barbecue when you had on those Madras shorts, the way they got all pushed up in there. All squishy."

"Clara you are not a nice person."

"Hmm." Tucking her chin to her chest, she seemed to fold up in the yards of crushed velvet.

Because it hadn't gone very well, and because she had another reading that evening – some type of group thing at the Knights of Columbus – Clara agreed to shave her fee. He paid her thirty-five plus grocery money. Telling her to leave out the back way.

"Sleep tight," she said giving him a phony friendly wave.

Russell slept poorly. At least with a warm omelette and some toast under his belt.

CHAPTER 6

Protecto

Come morning frost coated the grass and shrubs with a shimmering glaze – all was silver outside his window – the air, sky, everything still. He stood shivering in a flannel robe leftover from his college days (too tight now to cover his middle), watching a pair of squirrels cavort along the rim of the bird bath.

"I hope your nuts freeze in the ground before you ever get to eat them," Russell said. Let those squirrels know. Let them see what life is like without a proper food supply. Let them feel the deprivation.

The kind he was feeling. Though Clara did supply the food items he requested. Still. It wasn't the same. He enjoyed going to the market, skimming the shelves and choosing what to buy, putting things into the cart then carrying them home. It was his routine.

How long before the snows? Russell wondered. Wishing for perpetual blizzards he made the *Sign of the Cross.* Anything to weaken the squirrel population, starve them out. Obliterate the entire species if necessary. Gray ones, black ones, bushy tails, skinny tails. The whole stinking stupid furry lot of them. "OUT!!!"

Who cares if they're American squirrels or South American squirrels or Antarctica squirrels? As he gazed out the window even more appeared. Charging the garage roof, running the fence, swarming the yard. All capable of sudden unpredictable behavior. Russell scratched his armpit, the doubt creeping in again. Was it a squirrel? "It had to be!" he yelled into the silence.

A special suit was needed. So when it came time to leave the house he'd put on his protective covering and be ready.

His high school football helmet – it would practically take a bomb to blast through that. On the closet floor he found a pair of rubber boots that used to belong to his father. Hanging off hooks in the kitchen, two Teflon-coated oven mitts Maggie must've bought. Big and silver. He held them to his chest a moment; certain he felt heat; unable to determine the source of this sudden warmth. Was it coming out of him or the big mitts? Either way, it felt good. He pressed them closer.

Yesterday in her ramblings Clara mentioned something about warmth. Or was it pleasure? From the coat closet he took out his GOR-TEX jacket – hardly ever worn on account of its restrictive bulk.

Freedom of movement Russell used to believe. Freedom for all. And that included the animal kingdom. All that had changed.

Pants were the final item to complete his protective suit. *PROTECTO* came to mind. A good name. He'd seen it somewhere. Condoms? When was the last time he went to the drugstore and bought...? Shaking it off, he was thinking maybe he could market his *PROTECTO* in those ecology-type magazines. That would certainly qualify as employment. Even to Stan. Wasn't the whole world going totally out of whack? Who could predict what would be next? Even the squirrels were flipping out; Russell could verify *that* first hand.

Unable to locate any unusually heavy pants, he would have to make due with his winter-weight jeans. And hope for the best.

After breakfast he put on his *PROTECTO*, feeling a certain pride in his unique eco-concept. He tucked the football helmet under his arm. The boots being somewhat tricky – his father had had much larger feet. Forcing Russell to move slowly. In the powder room, with the *Bug Lite* making the mirror smeary yellow, he put on the football helmet. All in all, not quite *eco*; but pretty damned idiotic looking. Telling himself this was just the prototype. The final *PROTECTO* would surpass any shit the military could dream up.

He pushed back his shoulders feeling that sudden unexplained warmth again; this time streaming up from his toes into his groin and belly. It felt very good. Particularly his groin. He pushed his balls into a better position in the jeans. Nothing could get at him, break him, rip his skin. No more. Not the squirrel, not Maggie, not anything. Russell stepped outside.

Surveying the yard he decided it was a pretty good day. A bit grayish but what did that matter. He started toward the driveway when an itch seized his back. Deep and irrational. A killer itch. Wiggling his shoulders, he managed to mostly dislodge it. "Nothing worse when you're fully dressed for the outdoors," he said.

Swimmy in the big boots he started down the driveway, ducking a little when leaves rustled overhead.

CHAPTER 7

No Rescue

The next few days it rained steady. Soaked, his *PROTECTO* seemed to swell and double in weight. Twice while wearing it he stood under *the squirrel tree*: first for protection from the elements, the second time just for the heck of it. Later, he questioned his motives. Was it a test? To see if the squirrel might stage another attack? Or, to see if he could survive another one?

Under that dripping tree he was thinking Fig must live somewhere in the neighborhood. She might spot him getting drowned out here and invite him into her warm home. Though she probably had a Mr. Fig. At this point in life, thought Russell, most everyone did. No door opened. Nobody came out of any house to offer a hot morning coffee. Russell returned home without incident. Taking off the drenched clothes, he kicked them down the basement stairs. Two coffees later, finally warm in his too tight robe, he phoned Stan at work inviting him over for supper. His brother didn't sound all that enthusiastic.

"How 'bout I cook us a turkey?"

"You have a turkey?"

"Twelve pounder. In the freezer."

Stan made a sound like a wrench working a tight corner. "I s'pose."

Russell wanting to say: turkeys don't grow on trees, you know, a free-range bird costs *bucks*, a turkey takes hours of butter basting, then you have the gravy... swallowing all that he told Stan, "Come around six. And come 'round back."

"I know the drill."

CHAPTER 8

Half Deer Half Elk

Stan strolled into the kitchen swinging a bottle of partly used scotch, thumping it on the table. Some off-brand Russell never heard of, with an animal logo. Half-deer half-elk. Or maybe it was a moose stalking the dark-green label.

He gave Stan a nod by way of greeting, then bent to open the oven door.

"Turkey," said Stan. "Breast?"

"Full bird. Looking good, looking good. Say, where'd you come up with that brand of scotch?"

"Who knows? Somebody brought it to a barbecue. Maybe Clara." He chucked his jacket on a chair sniffing loudly. "That gobbler does smell good! Yeah, probably Clara, she shops cheap when it's a gift."

She's cheap in more ways than one, thought Russell, squirting melted butter from the turkey syringe down the crisp sides of the bird. He was still pissed. That crack she made about his Madras shorts. *All squishy up in there.* Clenching his toes he shut the oven door with a smack. "Clara is quite something to behold."

Stan chuckled. "That she is. She has the gift. You have to give her that much. She saved *my* life." He was opening and shutting cabinet doors. "Where do you keep the bar glasses, I can never remember."

"What do you mean she saved your life?"

"Just that. Clara saved me."

"Could you be a little more specific?"

Pouring scotch two-thirds up a tall, frosted-plastic glass, Stan took a noisy gulp. Russell about to comment it was more of an iced tea glass, when his brother said, "She saved me from marrying her. When I saw what a bitch she is. Like I said, Clara has the gift."

Russell had planned on steaming fresh cauliflower. Instead he took out a bag of frozen peas, adding water to a saucepan. "Are you saying the whole thing is a scam? That stuff she does with the cards?"

"It is and it isn't."

He could feel himself getting tight around the neck. "Be straight with me, Stan. I can't take much more. Nobody gives it to you straight. Maggie..." He was unable to go on. Adding another inch or so of water to the peas, he stood facing the tile backsplash. Rooster tiles, here and there, placed among tiles in solid yellow or red. Maggie was a rooster freak. A particular rooster, grouted in just above the sink spout, seemed especially cocky. Russell gave it a squirt from the turkey baster. "The thing is, I feel duped all the time. Can Clara really see into the future?"

"Not exactly."

He spun around facing his brother. "Then it is a scam!"

Stan, straddling a kitchen chair, flipped his Knicks cap backward. "There's more to it than just seeing into the future. Clara can set you on the right track."

"And what track might that be?"

Russell felt weak. He'd been feeling odd since the squirrel. He wanted to say that Clara was so far off the track she didn't know there was one. He didn't feel much like eating; was considering calling the whole thing off; donating the twelve pound turkey to the town Food Pantry, when Stan stood up and gave him a pat on the back. "Not to worry, bro. Clara sees a bright light ahead of you."

"I thought you said she can't see into the future."

"She's very good with the white light."

The kitchen was warm and savory. They ate saying very little. Stan easily consuming twice as much as Russell, who, by then, had completely lost his appetite. Plus his ability to speak. He felt stuck, hardly able to utter a word. His main reason for inviting Stan over was to discuss Fig. Now he couldn't even get her name out. Which wasn't her name anyway! For sure, Stan would have a thing or three to say about that. Frankly, Russell wasn't in the mood. Distracted, he nibbled at a wing while his brother ladled more and more gravy onto slabs of white meat.

"Stan, don't ever get married again."

"I don't need to, not with a bro who can cook like this. Man this turkey is terrific. You gettin' a cold? You sound congested." Stan picked up the scotch. "Want a splash?"

Russell coughed clearing his throat for the umpteenth time. "That's one sad looking elk you've got there." He put his turkey wing on the plate. "OK, pour me a shorty. So I meet this woman the other day, during the... squirrel incident." Russell had stopped saying out loud that the squirrel bit him. It was becoming murky territory.

His brother pouring three quarters up another frosted-plastic glass.

"Anyway, I can't get her out of my head. The woman from that... day. I swear I can smell her musk right this second. Right here in this kitchen."

"I smell turkey."

He took a gulp of scotch. "You know this really is an iced tea glass."

"Whatever."

"Stan, let me ask you something. Do you think Maggie was nice? I mean, was she what you'd call a nice person?"

His brother reached into the pocket of his flannel shirt taking out two cigars. "Nice? I'll give you a prime example. You tell me one woman who'd let you smoke a cigar at the table. Go on, name me one."

It's true, thought Russell. Maggie even making him give up cigarettes. She found a substitute type from the health food store made out of vegetables or possibly that disgusting tofu.

"Mom," said Russell. "There's a woman who lets you smoke at the table."

"You're talking a whole different generation. Their men trained them right from the get-go. In those days a man knew his place and made sure the woman knew hers." Stan was cutting the cigar. "Christ, can you picture Mom telling Pop not to smoke?"

"Never."

"By the way, I think it's about time for you to remodel this kitchen. The whole house needs an update. All that flowered furniture in the living room. And plastic slipcovers. What's that all about?" Stan blew out a blast of smoke. "What's with this rooster wallpaper? Roosters on the backsplash. I've never seen so many roosters in one place."

Holding his plastic glass of scotch Russell thought: Maggie. It's all about Maggie. The roosters, the flowered couch, the ugly oak, the damned plastic, the whole damned house. "She was a rooster freak. Collected them. She called them Country French." In a weird moment of deference to her Russell added, "Well she said Country French is trendy for home décor." He pointed toward the refrigerator. "Look at the one up top there."

"Whew," said Stan. "It's watching us."

What is it with these women and the whole Frenchie-thing? Clara, too – she had those French tarot cards.

"I think you'd like Fig," he told Stan.

"Figs. Yeah." He patted his stomach. "Good for the digestion."

CHAPTER 9

Bliss

A couple more trips outdoors in his *PROTECTO* and Russell called it quits. Retiring it permanently down the basement, along with his scheme to market to ecology magazines. He examined the oven mitts. One had developed a small rip that expanded to a hole during the turkey roasting.

"Useless pieces of crap," he said chucking them in the trash. Suddenly anxious to be rid of anything remotely Maggie. *Magpie*, Stan used to say behind her back. Also: *I am not an animal* – from the Elephant Man movie.

He took the rooster off the top of the refrigerator dumping that in the trash, too.

Stan had a point. It was time. Rip down the rooster wallpaper and give the kitchen a coat of fresh paint. For sure the place needed updating. Change. Russell reflecting on the nasty rooster faces, the cocky tilt to their crooked beaks. Besides, he was feeling restless; it would give him something to do. Again during dinner Stan mentioned the fact of the Gulf War being over a long time. Long enough to start a few more new wars, thought Russell, picking at a loose corner of wallpaper. It peeled about an inch then held on tight.

Leaving the house cautiously, he made the walk into town under partly sunny skies. He bought a newspaper. The trip back was uneventful.

❧

At the kitchen table he spread out the paper to the classifieds. Nothing much. Waiters, bus boys, sales jobs, computer tech. He didn't own a computer. *Landscaper*. That particular listing making him feel unhinged. Only one caught his interest, and only slightly. One he felt qualified to pursue: Driver. However, he no longer owned a car.

The listing said you needed your own wheels. He used to have a turquoise Mustang, '65 classic. He sold it around the time his disability kicked in. Stan had hollered like hell saying *How could you let that car go being mint and all.* Russell said he got sick of the color. Turquoise inside and out. That it started to nauseate him. In a way it was true. Plus he was seeing himself as a more neutral type of car owner. Something in sleek silver-gray. Not to mention that selling the car brought in a nice chunk of change. He never did get around to replacing the Mustang. He liked walking. The small downtown just a ten to fifteen minute walk. Depending on how fast you went; and whether or not you got bit by a squirrel.

❧

The days were growing shorter. More and more squirrels came out of wherever they hid, making more and more of a mess out of his grass. And Stan kept calling the squirrel *just one of those things.*

No, thought Russell, not anymore. No more *things.* I want my bliss.

On TV he'd seen this docudrama where a woman claimed to be following her bliss. At the time it seemed kind of corny. The trees shimmered with golden leaves making a canopy over the woman who was barefoot, and of course beautiful, while pointed shafts of light filtered down onto a stone city where the woman seemed to float through arched alcoves. In and out she floated, in and out; her long white dress sheer, almost see-through. The whole thing was stupid yet somehow peaceful. He'd seen it around the time Maggie left. It reminded him of Venice. Those old crumbling cities. Except he'd never been to any. Only to the Middle East, and that was no bliss.

I'm starving, thought Russell. He didn't want turkey leftovers. He didn't want the German bologna wrapped tightly in Saran. Not even fresh Oreos dunked in milk. "What do I want?" he yelled into the silent kitchen.

CHAPTER 10

Power Lines

That night he phoned the DRIVER listing in the paper. A machine picked up and he left his number.

It felt silly, almost ridiculous. They used to call them *chauffeurs*. Very hoity toity. He wondered if he'd have to wear a uniform? Russell had despised his army uniform, especially the winter one that made every inch of him itchy. Maybe he could get by as a driver by just wearing a peaked cap. But he was getting ahead of himself. The interview wasn't even set up. At least that gave him prep time. He thought about phoning Clara, see if she could lay any psychic insights on him. Instead he phoned his mother at the assisted living facility. She nagged him about not visiting and drove him crazy in under five minutes. He hung up and called Stan. When he mentioned phoning Clara for her insights, his brother told him to forget it.

"Why?"

"Practically everything Clara knows she learned from a computer course on how to become a psychic."

"What! You told me she was good! At least with the white light."

"Only face to face. She's no good on the phone, something goes blooey. Probably on account of the power lines. I don't know. Over the phone she can give it to you backwards."

Backwards. That he could do by himself. Or, so he'd been told.

Was Stan using this power line argument because he happened to be an electrical engineer? People could be protective when it came to their area of expertise, thinking no one else could get it right.

With the phone to his ear, Russell peered over the café curtains on the sink window. Daylight was waning while roosters pranced along the curtain's blue border. Scanning for squirrels, and seeing plenty, he grabbed the valance ripping it down rod and all.

"What's that racket?" said Stan.

"Did Clara read you backwards on the phone?"

"Me? She never read me. She said she got it off me like looking at a picture."

CHAPTER 11

Exterminator

In the car service office, a forty-something woman, perched on a stool behind the counter, stared intently at a computer screen. Her roughened face had a sleep deprived look that reminded Russell of a fence past its prime. In a strange way, enticing. Her skin and hair were dark like Fig's but this woman looked more sun ripened. Not exactly a prune – though her future could be risky. She seemed the type to do the freighter travel thingy in her twenties, when it was still a cool thing to do.

Formerly a gas station, the car service office had been stripped of its pumps, its bay area empty of cars needing fixing. The dingy cramped office felt damp and chilly and stank like a million cigarettes. Reflexively he coughed. The woman looked up from the computer. Zipped to the neck in his khaki jacket a shiver ran through Russell. He didn't know if it was her eyes or the place that was giving him the heebie-jeebies. Unnatural emerald green, those eyes seemed to cut right through you. Contacts? Had to be. All wrong for her face. Startling in a bad way.

He lifted one hand by way of greeting. "Hi, I'm Russell. I phoned and left a message about the driver job." Then he wanted to turn around and leave. She hadn't opened her mouth, yet he felt like he'd been left bloodless.

Frowning, pursing her lips, she looked him up and down a few times like inspecting for termites. An exterminator, he thought. Another female exterminator.

She tilted her head in a coy way. "I was expecting a much younger man. But now that you're here..."

How much younger? he thought. In diapers?

"Are you fit?" she said.

He shoved his hands in his pockets. "I can drive a car. If that's what you mean."

"What type of vehicle are we talking about?"

She meant *his* car. “I don’t exactly own a car at the moment.”

“Then why did you answer the listing?”

“I thought we might be able to work something out.”

When he first walked in, he noticed the mini American flag sticking out of a water glass, behind her, on a shelf attached to the pegboard wall – it seemed like an omen – that little flag.

“I happen to be a veteran of The Gulf War,” said Russell keeping the flag in his peripheral vision. “Desert Storm.”

She smiled, one front tooth overlapping the other. Like little arms, he thought smiling back at her, instinctively placing his one hand on top of the other, in front of him. She noticed and her smile faded. Did she take this as some form of mimicry on account of her teeth? Who knows? He dropped his arms to his sides.

“That war part sounded rehearsed.” She made a clicking noise with her mouth. “Whatever. I’m Nina. I own this place.”

“I did serve in the war!”

“Whatever, like I said. So you think owning this place is a man’s job? Ha! Never mind. Don’t answer.”

“I didn’t say that.”

“As a matter of fact I might be able to use you. I’ve got a driver with a bum leg at the moment who’s got this newish Lincoln Continental that’s going to waste.” She made a *tsk tsk* sound. “Maybe you can lease it from him. I don’t know.” Turning back to the computer she acted like the whole thing didn’t matter.

When Russell said nothing in return, she picked up a little steam. “Triple black. Very sleek. Good for driving celebrities who don’t want to be seen. Anonymous celebrities.” She let out a big horsey laugh. “That’s becoming a rarer and rarer event. You want coffee?”

He accepted, thanking her. Coffee is quite civilized, maybe this will turn out OK, he thought, watching her fiddling with the coffee maker. “Milk?” she said. It took at least another ten minutes for the coffee to come out. “Should have sprung for the deluxe model,” was all she said.

Finally cradling the cardboard cup, he took a stool at the counter facing her. There was still the matter of his disability. He’d have to find a way of telling Nina he needed to get paid under the table. Make a little joke of it – say it while giving the counter a slap; since they were already at the counter having their cups of coffee.

He took a sip then ditched the idea. Acting cute with this woman might not go over. Resting the cup on his knee he smiled a little sad smile. "You see, I'm on disability at the moment."

"And it's about to run out?" Her face took on that squinty expression like she expected a swarm at any moment.

"I was hoping we could work out an arrangement."

"Wait a minute! First you have no car, now you're telling me you want cash under the table?"

"Under the counter?" He gave it a light whack thinking *what the fuck.*

Nina took a step back. "I don't know. That stuff can be risky." She ran a finger across the countertop. "Dust. This place gets so dusty. I don't know where it comes from. A kind of white dust." She held up her finger staring at it. "Strange, don't you think? I hate filth. Do you smoke?"

"No way." For once he was grateful to Maggie for making him quit; though it choked him to admit it.

"Well that's something anyway. The cars get ruined if you smoke. You may as well junk them for scrap. Leo would go after you with a tire iron if you ruined his car. You *capeesh* what I'm telling you?"

"Nina, I do not smoke."

"So what's your disability? Physical?" Those glittery green eyes working him over.

He squirmed on the stool.

"Mental?'

"Under the veteran's Privacy Act I'm under no obligation..."

"Never mind, never mind, we'll talk tomorrow," she said.

❧

Early that evening, enjoying salami and chopped celery on rye, surrounded by the strutting roosters, Russell began feeling a little better. Better than he had in a long time. He touched his neck where the squirrel bit him; lately an almost unconscious gesture. Nina hadn't offered him the job. Nothing had changed. Still. He felt OK.

CHAPTER 12

Blank

"Leo is willing to make a deal," said a voice over the phone. A female voice. Russell rubbed sleep from his eyes.

"Leo?"

"My other driver?"

"Right!" He threw his legs over the side of the bed sitting up in the pitch dark. "What time is it?"

"Hey Russell – if you're one of those early-to-bed-late-to-rise types you won't cut it in this business."

"Nooo! Not at all. I only went to bed early because I have to be up at the crack of dawn. Before dawn, actually."

"Oh really? For what reason?"

"Fishing. I'm going *down the shore.* The blues are running and I'm going with my brother, Stan. Our annual fall fishing trip."

There was silence.

"Nina? Are you there?"

"See me the day after tomorrow." The phone going dead.

Russell fell back on the bed and let out a yawn. Driver. He thought about what that might mean, and came up blank.

CHAPTER 13

Fishy

A ponytail guy, sitting slumped at the counter of the car service office, was doing his best to ignore Russell. Despite that he jingled change in his pocket, then coughed, then said *Excuse me* to the guy. Finally he leaned over the counter. "I'm here to see Nina."

"You want Nina?"

"Yeah. I'm here to iron out a few small details."

"I'll bet."

"You wouldn't happen to be Leo?"

The guy made an almost imperceptible nod. Hostile, thought Russell. He had that same weather-beaten face she had. Could it be from the florescent lighting? Making the place too bright white. He heard somewhere that over time those lights can zap your health.

"Sis!" Leo called out just as Nina came trotting around the pegboard wall.

"Catch any fish?"

A brother and sister! That explains the matching bad skin. "So you two are related." He couldn't come up with anything better.

"She's my big sis." Leo grinned putting an arm across her shoulders. Nina's eyes brightening greener. Gumball-eyes, thought Russell. Turn your tongue green for a week.

Nina was saying, "I take care of my boy. I watch out for what's mine." She smiled at Leo, then swung her gaze at Russell, looking him over top to bottom, though not as ominously as the last time.

"You two talk," she said. "Remember, this is only temporary! As soon as Leo's leg is healed and he can work the pedals, he gets the car back. Capeesh? I don't want to have to put this in writing!"

Russell flinched. In writing! I don't think so.

This Nina was quite the savvy little businesswoman. The last thing *he* needed was any written record of employment. "Not to worry," he assured the brother and sister. "By that time I'll probably have my own Lincoln."

Neither said a word.

❧

It was agreed that Russell should begin immediately, which meant that afternoon. A dark suit, or blue blazer and slacks would serve as his uniform. No hat required. Limping badly, Leo took him outside to see the car. As they rounded the building, a Doberman threw itself repeatedly against the chain link fence that marked its pen.

"It can't get out, right?" Russell eyed the jaw opening and closing.

"Geek! Quiet!" The dog slinking back.

The Lincoln was good looking – for a big old boat from the late 'nineties. Russell taking in the gleaming black paint and chrome trim shining like aluminum foil. Spotless smoky tinted windows. He poked his head inside. The black interior immaculate.

"Leather?" He sniffed.

"Top grade. I find one cigarette burn on these seats..."

"Leo, please. Like I told Nina I don't smoke. Never have." A little white lie under the circumstances... Leo definitely the type to come after you with a hunk of heavy metal such as Nina mentioned.

"I'll treat this car with the respect it deserves."

Leo sort of moaned, dropping the tough guy role. "She's all I've got."

"I hear you, bro." It occurred to him that he just said *bro*. Stan's word. Stan always doing the big brother bit. He was doing the same with Leo. "Don't worry, everything will be OK," Russell told him.

Leo patted the fender. "This is Russell, he'll be your new master."

Master? What kind of psycho shit? thought Russell rubbing his chin. What could cause a man to lose his grip this way? The dog began barking again as Nina came strutting toward them. "So you've met the goddess. But have you fallen in love?"

"She's a beautiful piece of equipment!" Leo sounding wounded.

"Just trying to keep things light."

What is it with these women? Russell was thinking. Why do they always have to emasculate the male? Stan liked saying: It's nicer on the bottom where it's warmer and you don't have to work so hard. Well Maggie sure didn't get that point. She always wanted tops and ended up doing most of the hard labor. God knows what, or who, she's doing now.

CHAPTER 14

Messages

As he was knotting his maroon polyester-silk tie (tie is optional Nina said) he heard Stan's voice on the answering machine. He grabbed the portable phone.

"I'm kind of in a hurry."

"I've got two messages for you, bro."

"Is it Mom?"

"They're from Clara."

Inwardly Russell groaned.

"She said to tell you to expect mountains."

What the fuck mountains? "Yeah, OK, tell her OK." He chuckled to himself thinking I'll watch out for mountains at Newark Airport.

"Her second message was for you to *proceed cautiously.* Wait, let me get this exact. I wrote it down. She insisted. Here we go. She said: *Tell Russell to proceed with caution.* She even made me read it back to her."

"Was this on the phone?"

"Yeah, this morning."

"You said Clara is no good on the phone."

"She told me you'd say that."

His tie looked crooked. "Stan, I've got to go."

"She told me you'd say that, too."

Already more than two messages. "Talk to you later."

Adjusting his tie in the bedroom mirror, the machine came on again. This time he heard Nina telling him to pack a light bag. Cautiously, he lifted the portable from its cradle. "Can you explain what you mean by pack a light bag?"

"The funniest thing!" She was laughing, all giggly-girl sounding. "My friend Beverly, who owns another car service, well, she couldn't accommodate this guy. She phoned to see if I could. Turns out he's Billy Bud Wilcox."

When Russell was silent she said, "The country western singer? Come alive, man! You're going to drive him home for the holidays."

What holidays? Thanksgiving was still a month off. "Where does he live?"

"Colorado."

"Colorado! That's probably a four, five day car trip! Can't he take a plane?"

"Fear of flying. His entire band went down in a crash, one of those small planes that hit a mountain during a snowstorm." She paused. "Such a shame."

"A plane crash!"

"Yeah. Anyway come by the office and pick up the maps. You can read a map, right? You must know north from south, east from west. You were in the army. Right?"

He clenched his toes in his loafers. Stan said Clara mentioned mountains... Now this Nina is talking about a small plane...

"Russell? Right?"

"Yes I was in the army," he answered robotically. His eyes skimmed the walls. His cozy bedroom. Maggie had painted it lavender-blue, then stenciled a cloud border near the ceiling. "This is kind of short notice," he said. "What about a GPS? Also I have pets, you know."

"What – cats, dogs, birds? A hamster? Leo can feed them and walk them if necessary."

"Actually..."

"Don't tell me it's an iguana! Leo has a deep fear of snakes."

Since when is an iguana a snake? thought Russell. "Actually they're tropical fish." He didn't say *mostly guppies*, that the rare tropical fish were long gone. "They need feeding and require constant care. There's the water level and temperature to be checked, and the tank gets inspected for algae and cleaned twice a week." That part was a lie; he barely cleaned it once a week.

"Leo can do all that." She sounded annoyed. "When you applied for this job you had no car, you had *that other issue* (she lowered her voice), but you didn't mention entanglements!" Her voice had risen sharply at the end.

Entanglements? He'd never viewed his fish as anything that complicated. Though perhaps in a way they were. "Well, I am fond of them."

"Russell can I count on you to drive Billy Bud Wilcox to Colorado?"

"No GPS?"

"Nope."

He swallowed. "You can count on me, Nina."

As soon as he hung up, he phoned Stan. "I'm going to Colorado. I'm taking Billy Bud Wilcox. I'm his driver. I'm working for a car service. No GPS."

"What! You're driving Billy Bud Wilcox, that old country western singer? I thought he was dead. Well I'll be damned. When'd you get this job?"

"Day before yesterday. I think." He couldn't quite remember. "Look, can you come by and feed my fish, do the tank stuff? Nina's got this half-wit brother she wants to let loose on my house."

"Who the hell is Nina?"

"My new boss."

CHAPTER 15

Rocky Mountain High

Colorado. He was clueless about that part of the country. It did have mountains though; as in Clara's message. People did go skiing in Colorado. That was the sum total of his knowledge. *Rocky Mountain High.*

Colorado must be freezing this time of year, he thought, pulling off his socks and changing into a thicker winter pair while mulling over the squirrel situation out west. Did they have fatter squirrels on account of the colder weather? He pictured the Colorado squirrels stuffing themselves all summer in preparation for what was to come.

Taking his duffel bag from the hall closet, Russell packed long underwear as well as regular, more thick socks, white tee shirts, a wool sweater, flannel PJ's, two flannel shirts, jeans and a baseball hat. More than enough. For a moment his *PROTECTO* flickered through his mind. Nina would never approve. Besides, it was too bulky for driving. He wouldn't be able to move his arms to turn the wheel of the Lincoln. If Billy Bud Wilcox asked him a question, from the back seat, he wouldn't be able to turn his head, even slightly (not that you want to turn around much while you're driving to Colorado).

Russell grabbed his only overcoat, a navy-blue wool. Maggie bought it as a present some time before he went to The Gulf. It always reminded him of what undertakers wore – standing next to the hearse waiting for the coffin.

CHAPTER 16

Cards... again

At the car service office Nina was all sparkly in a glitter headband and green reindeer sweater that matched her eyes. Intentional? Kind of early for *the season* Russell was thinking – by a few months.

"This is a big ticket job!" she was saying looking flushed in the cheeks. "You'll make some good money. Play your cards right you'll get a big fat tip from Billy Bud Wilcox."

Cards again, he was thinking.

She brandished a rag, began rubbing the glass counter. "Smears. I hate when people lean. Why do they have to lean?" She looked up, those green eyes were like glass shards cutting him. "You have a Visa card, right? Tell me you have a Visa, Russell."

"Why?"

"Why? Because you'll have to sleep in a few motels along the way. Did you expect to sleep in the car?"

"I have to pay?"

"Billy Bud Wilcox will pay." She let out a long sigh. "He'll pay for everything. Rooms, food, gas, band aids. *What-ever*. Your Visa is a back up. In case something goes wrong. You never know."

"Like what?"

"I don't know!" She threw him a look, going at the smears even more strenuously. "Life is unpredictable. You never know."

What did he never know? Would banditos hold him at gunpoint along the route?

Choosing his words carefully he said, "This isn't Mexico, Nina." A recent news report about that country advised people to abandon their car if they had the misfortune to get a flat.

Now she was cleaning down the sides of the counter, using a spray that reeked of ammonia.

"Can't you give me an advance? In case something does go

wrong? I will get reimbursed, right? I don't like to depend on other people's money." Feeling anxious, Russell rubbed his hands together.

"What other people? Ahhh... nice and clean now. Oh you mean the money. It's all factored in. To Billy Bud Wilcox's bill," she said in her smooth way.

"Yeah?"

"Basically what you're getting is an all expense paid vacation." She stepped behind the counter to rummage in a drawer, handing him a slip of paper. "Here's his address. I'll call and say you'll be there in ten minutes."

Russell looked around the small office. The army fed him that same line of bull: See the world for free. The *reserves* had been a huge mistake. At least they threw in some added perks like the VA Medical System. The last time Russell stopped by the VA for his flu shot, another Vet in the crowded waiting area told him: You might as well jump off a bridge.

"Where's Leo?" Where's *the gimp*?

"Bringing the car around front."

"By the way, Nina, my brother Stan will feed my fish. So you don't have to worry about that part." Adding quickly, "Not that I wouldn't trust Leo one hundred percent."

Her face got that scrunched look. "I'm sure."

CHAPTER 17

P-3

Billy Bud Wilcox lived in the only high rise apartment building in the area. It stuck up into the sky, a white tower among single family houses and a low slung shopping center.

"You'll be wanting the Penthouse." The bored looking doorman seemed sleepy at his post.

When Russell just stood there staring at a fountain bubbling chartreuse water, the doorman said, "You must be new. You have to go up there and bring Mr. Wilcox down. P-3."

He took the elevator to P. It opened to P-3. No other doors were visible. He wondered how many apartments took up the Penthouse floor? He rang the buzzer for P-3. It went off deep in the bowels of the apartment belonging to BBW. He'd started thinking of the country western singer as BBW. It felt easier. Billy Bud Wilcox was a mouthful.

He heard steps, then the door was opened by a thin elderly woman with gray hair piled in a bun. About to ask if she was Mrs. Wilcox, the woman said, "Mr. Billy is almost ready. Won't you come in and have a seat."

So! Old Billy Bud Wilcox, or old BBW, or old Mr. Billy has a maid! *Mr. Billy* reminded him of a goat. The place did look very clean and tidy, maybe *Mr. Billy* ate the garbage. Russell smirking at his little joke.

Though he had to admit, all in all, it was a pretty nice place. The expensive looking furniture a tad gaudy. Too much red. But the old guy would have been weaned at the Grand Ole Opry. Russell had seen pictures of the stage lit up red. Personally, he wouldn't mind having a maid. It would take a lot of the pressure off. He doubted he'd ever be able to afford one. Nina would make a good maid, always rubbing at some smudge you couldn't see. Fig would not make a good maid. Something felt messy around her. Maybe it was her scent – that couldn't be contained; drifting past his mind when he least expected.

He heard a voice call out something. Too high pitched to be a man's voice. The same voice repeating what Russell now heard distinctly. "I'm getting tired of this crap!" Billy Bud Wilcox? Not a good sign. This scenario could be tricky. Driving an old crazy man, even a famous one, all the way to Colorado, made Russell uneasy. Could the whole thing be a set up? Nina and Leo, aware the old singer was nuts, had staged Leo's bum leg; to save Leo's sorry ass. Nina did say *I look after my boy* or something like that.

The maid came back smiling saying Mr. Billy was almost ready. A smile of relief? Russell wondered. The old gal glad to get the old pisser out of her hair for the holidays?

"You'll like Mr. Billy," she said. "Everyone does."

Uh-huh he was about to answer out of politeness, when the shrill voice shrieked again. "I'm getting tired of this crap!"

He stared at the maid.

"That's just Marilyn Monroe, Mr. Billy's mynah bird. Marilyn always gets mad when he has to leave. He tells her he's coming back, but she never believes him." The maid shrugged. "Issues, I guess."

"I guess!" Russell greatly relieved it was a bird and not the man in question.

There was some shuffling, then Mr. Billy – or Billy Bud Wilcox – or BBW appeared in the hall. His snow white hair still thick, his grin still *pure country*. Everything about him pretty much as Russell remembered from the record albums and TV appearances. Except now he was frail, leaning on a walker. His camel hair overcoat almost trailing the floor and billowing like it belonged to a much larger man. This man moved at a snail's pace.

Russell felt terror grip him by the neck. Only here was no squirrel. At this pace the days could stretch into weeks.

"How de do," the old man said, his deep set blue eyes riveted on Russell. More shuffling toward the door, pushing his walker, BBW called out a heartfelt goodbye. "Cheerio, old girl."

Whether this was meant for the maid, or Marilyn Monroe, was anyone's guess.

"I saw you on TV once with Dolly Parton," said Russell trying to establish a rapport.

"Bunk! I was on TV two dozen times with Dolly."

Nodding at the maid as she handed over BBW's suitcase, Russell followed behind in baby steps.

CHAPTER 18

Winner

It took a while to get the old man settled into the back seat of the Lincoln. He asked for the seat warmer to be turned on, and that took Russell some time, first to locate, never mind operate. He asked for the headrest to be lowered, and the front seat to be moved forward. He needed help with his seat belt over the bulky camel hair coat. All that took time. Then Russell had to chuck the walker and suitcase into the trunk. As he was finally pulling out of the circle driveway, a blast of cold air hit him on back of his neck. Billy Bud Wilcox had lowered the rear window.

"Is anything the matter?" Russell asked. Could he be car sick already?

"I like air," the old man said.

"Air is good," said Russell. "But it is winter, and winter is cold. You don't want to catch your de..." stopping himself short.

"Catch my what?"

"Well, you could catch a cold. Or sinusitis, or even bronchitis with the window open."

"It's not *winner*, yet. I'll close it when it's officially *winner.* December 21 is still the first day of *winner*, ain't that right? Unless they changed that too while I wasn't lookin'."

Kill me now thought Russell, turning up the collar on his blue blazer.

CHAPTER 19

Pit Stop

After about an hour's driving, they made a rest stop along the Jersey Turnpike so BBW could take a pee break. At least the concession area was warm. The old man had insisted on keeping his window cracked.

Despite that Russell turned the car heater up full blast, his neck and head were stiff from the cold blowing in. He felt like two different body systems shoved into one mass: half warm-blooded, half cold. He'd seen a TV show about some creature with that syndrome. Water snakes? The last time he felt this uncomfortable was in the army.

At the urinal BBW was having a hard time. He moved his walker this way and that. Russell wasn't about to step in, telling himself: I'm not his nurse-maid, just his driver. And why wasn't the old guy traveling with a nurse or even that maid? If they have to stop like this every hour, it will take forever to reach Colorado. Already Russell was losing patience.

"How 'bout a foot-long hot dog while we're here." At last swiveling his walker away from the urinal, the old man was grinning at Russell. "I noticed them grillin' those doggies on the way in. See this way we won't need to make a lunch stop. If you catch my drift."

Hmm. Russell somewhat cheered by the old guy's reasoning – that he still had reasoning; at least when it came to food. Maybe things wouldn't be so bad, now that he took his pee and was about to have his *hot doggie.* Maybe the day would move along smoothly. But something had to be done about that open window, or it was guaranteed pneumonia for both of them.

BBW ate two foot-long dogs, fries topped with ketchup mounded like *a mountain* (it didn't escape Russell's notice), washing it all down with a large Coke. It took him a long time to eat. Then so long to get his wallet out of his big coat that in the end Russell paid. Pocketing the receipt, and hoping this wasn't going to become a pattern. Another visit to the Mens Room. Finally settled in the car, Russell heard the back window sliding down.

Oh no you don't, he thought.

He'd discovered the main control located right there on his own door panel. The moment the window was fully down, Russell brought it back up; locking it.

Pressing on the window lever BBW practically burst a blood vessel. "I need my air! Release that latch!"

Russell hit the radio knob till he found a country music station, hoping it would quiet things down. The old guy shouted a few more obscenities before he shut up. Through the rear view mirror Russell could see BBW's mouth hanging open, the old watery eyes shut tight. Lowering the radio, he drove to the sounds of intermittent snoring.

The old man slept. And, slept. The Lincoln quite toasty now, the roomy leather front seat pretty comfortable. All in all. Russell had marked out the map route in a red line. From time to time he glanced down at it neatly folded on the passenger seat. Several hours later he had to make a pit stop of his own. By then they had crossed into Pennsylvania, the trees still blazing their oranges, reds and gold.

CHAPTER 20

Food and Lodging

When Russell returned to the car the old man was wide awake and railing. "Where'd you go? Where are we? You left me alone! Leaving a helpless man alone in a cold car! You should be ashamed!"

Unbuttoning his coat Russell choked back a laugh. "You, helpless? Give me a break. Nobody would dare come near this car. Besides, the windows are tinted, you can't really see in. Anyway I locked you in."

"What! You locked me in, are you insane? Nobody locks Billy Bud Wilcox in, nowhere! Turn this *mother* around. I'm goin' back."

Russell felt something snap against his skull. He swiveled in the front seat to face the old man. "What just hit my head?"

The rheumy eyes were smoldering, then a grin broke out across the wrinkled face. BBW held up a finger. "I *pinged* you."

"Don't do it again, Billy!"

"Who gave you permission to call me by my Christian name?"

"What should I call you?"

"Mister Wilcox. You're workin' for me. Only it don't seem too clear to you."

He's right. I am working for him, thought Russell. "OK. Mr. Wilcox. Can we get going now? It's almost dark and I still have to find us a motel."

"I only stay at Radisson or Intercontinental. In a pinch I'll slum at the Sheraton."

Russell felt the foot-long hot dog start to do a jig in his belly. "We're out in the boondocks. We have to take what we can get. A billboard a few miles back said there was food and lodging up ahead."

"Food and lodging! Do I look like a food and lodging type a guy? I need my comforts! You *unnerstand*? I won't take anyplace that doesn't have a whirlpool bathtub and designer body wash."

I sure do *unnerstand*. It's *winner* outside this car and I'm beginning to *unnerstand* a lot. Silently he cursed Nina and Leo. He cursed Maggie, his mother, the army, Stan for ragging him about finding a job, Clara and her cards, and finally the squirrel. Fig he did not curse. She was all he had. He closed his eyes a moment, her scent drifting past like a broken cloud.

❧

It wasn't Radisson or Intercontinental or even a Sheraton. "Not even a lousy Sheraton!" BBW was sputtering mad.

Just off the road, they were stopped next to a two-story, dark wood, no-tell-motel; the sort of place that meandered under heavy tree cover. Eyeing the pines suspiciously Russell pulled up closer to the building, near blue neon that spelled out OFFICE vertically. The cold blue light casting an even more gloomy spell over the place.

"You took me to the *Bates Motel*," said BBW.

Don't I wish, he thought, picturing the old man, instead of that blond, behind the shower curtain. "It's just for one night," he said opening the car door.

"Maybe the last night of my life. I never! This is some big come down."

Russell opened the back door. "Aw, Mr. Wilcox, I'm sure you stayed in places like this when you and your band went touring around the country."

"Never! My bus was custom-outfitted! Right down to the tufted satin Beautyrest mattress and percale sheets. This place..." he flapped his hands. "This place is a freakin' dive."

Stubbornly refusing the arm Russell extended into the car. "I'm not stayin' here, pal."

He knew something like this was going to happen. The old man chirped, "What the hell's wrong with your arms? Pretty damned short, I'd say."

With his arm still in the car, Russell froze. I don't have to take this abuse, he thought pulling it out. He stood there crouching a little under the thick trees. He could smell pine; also dampness and rot. The old wooden structure connected and cockeyed like a derailed train. It made him nostalgic. Those Catskill Mountain resorts – he and Stan had gone with their parents every summer for a week. Years later, he'd taken Maggie up there to The Black Swan, his favorite of them all. She despised the place, crapping all over it, saying it had *no nice carpet*.

Hearing movement overhead he tensed his shoulders, looking

up into the wild tangle of foliage; while other noises came from inside the car. BBW. Cursing out his fury.

"This is our home for the night. Home sweet home. See – *Vacancy*. I'm going in to register." He might have driven a little further, tried finding something better. Not now. Brushing a mottled leaf off the fender.

CHAPTER 21

Not That Way

The desk clerk assigned connecting rooms. Russell had hoped to be as far away as possible from the old man. And to make matters worse, BBW was insisting on leaving the door between the rooms open. Just getting him in the room had been a big production. Slumped on the bed wearing his coat the old man was yipping and complaining. “I want a porterhouse steak.”

I want a cyanide capsule, thought Russell. He put up his hands. “OK. OK. Wait here and I’ll go check on the food situation.”

Not bothering to lock either door he hurried out praying someone might abduct BBW; or spirit him away. He was now totally convinced that Nina and Leo were in cahoots. He wasn’t the driver so much as the babysitter. He practically had to wipe drool off the old guy’s chin.

Behind the counter a young woman told him, “Sorry, but our restaurant isn’t open in the off-season.” She had one of those blank, shut down faces. Did it open up during the on-season?

His little joke. He needed one. Russell shoved his hands in his pockets looking around. The place about as bare-bones as it gets. You don’t look sorry, he was thinking about the young woman. “So what you’re saying is that this place is some kind of resort? You have an on-season?”

She bobbed her head, two straw colored pig-tails bouncing on her rounded shoulders. “*In season.*” The little girl corrected him. “Didn’t you notice the lake?” she said.

He turned toward the window partially covered by dark drapes. “I didn’t see any lake here.”

“Not that way.” Lifting her eyebrows as if to say *Are you dense* the girl added, “Behind the building and down the trail.”

How could he be expected to see a lake that’s behind the motel and down a trail? Tired from driving he flexed his shoulders. Hadn’t seen anyone in pig-tails since the ‘seventies. Soon after, they went out of style – unless you raised hogs for a living. He looked around for a chair, not finding one. He still had to deal with dinner. He was so beat he could easily skip. Hit the sack early. You know that ain't gonna happen, Russell was thinking. "May I ask where the nearest restaurant is?"

"They're all closed for..."

"Right. The off-season."

The girl smiled coyly. "There's always the diner."

Always the diner. Clenching his toes in his loafers, he tried his best to smile back. "And where might the diner be?"

After her somewhat sketchy directions, then trudging back to the room, another struggle convincing BBW to get back in the car. While Russell was off negotiating the dinner plan, the old man had gotten sleepy. Still in the oversized camel coat he sprawled on top of the bedspread demanding Russell phone room service.

"Have 'em bring me a hamburger medium-rare with lettuce and pickles. A real burger. None of that veggie burger junk! On a see-same bun. No French fries. Lotsa ketchup. A Doctor Pepper. No! Ginger Ale."

See-same! Gritting his teeth Russell pressed *room service* on the phone. That BBW had led a charmed life, and enjoyed throwing his weight around, was becoming more and more apparent.

The cheery voice that answered "Room Service!" he recognized as belonging to the pig-tail girl.

"Nope," she replied when he asked about ordering food.

Russell hung up. Making his voice neutral he said, "There's no room service here. We have to eat out. At the diner. It's not far." He didn't know how far, or quite where to find it.

BBW made a squealing noise. Reclined against the knotty-pine headboard he was struggling to sit up. "Mother of God," he said. "Will ya look at this room. Institution green. I feel like I went to jail. I feel like I died."

You're not the only one, thought Russell. Then deciding he better try and jolly-up the old guy, he smiled. "Hey, Mr. Wilcox. Did you ever write a song like that one by Johnny Cash, about the Folsom Prison?"

BBW sniffed. "A criminal with a small talent."

"Johnny Cash? I think a lot of people wouldn't agree with that."

"I want my food," said BBW.

CHAPTER 22

Pink in Candlelight

The diner was way below average but to Russell's amazement the old man didn't seem to notice. Or at least kept quiet about it. Eating methodically, alternating bites of burger with gulps of Root Beer. He didn't make a scene when the waitress told him they had no Ginger Ale, or Doctor Pepper, or cat piss soda. Russell admired the way she threw *cat piss soda* right back at the old man saying, "No cat piss soda tonight, sorry."

BBW seemed strangely calm. He must've slipped into an *alternate state*; perhaps induced while he was alone in the room; while Russell was conversing with Miss Piggly-Wiggly-Tails. Out of nowhere he felt horny. He wondered how old she was. The pig-tails aside, she looked young. Jail bait? He took a bite of his sandwich. Now there's a word hadn't crossed his mind or lips in about thirty years. Johnny Cash's fault. Did the other more famous country singer ever sample jail bait? Russell decided the answer was *yes*, a definite yes. He looked at BBW over his BLT on toast, about to ask his opinion on that subject, when the old man glanced up. "What is it?" Cranky again.

"I was just wondering about something, nothing in particular." Russell coughed on the dry bacon. As for the old coot, it was hard to imagine him with any woman, even a mature woman. In the booth, he seemed to have shrunk. "Have you ever been married?" he asked BBW.

The old eyes glinted steely. "Six. I wed five fillies. The last one don't count."

"I'm sorry, I don't understand."

"That one turned out to be a gelding."

Confused, Russell shook his head.

"Sonny, I married a woman in the process of convertin' her plumbing." He turned soft around the mouth then. "Too bad," he whispered, "that one was my favorite. I woulda kept that one.

Shelley Lee Wilcox. Tiny little thing. Prettiest red hair you ever saw. Her bush, too, a real fire bush. So much red it looked pink in candlelight."

Russell didn't know what to say. Pink in candlelight. It made him uncomfortable. Plus it was the longest speech yet to come out of Billy Bud Wilcox. He thought of Maggie, how she'd been his *one and only;* while this coot up and married six women! Well, five – since Billy didn't count the one in transition. Kind of like the squirrel. Russell still harboring suspicions over its gender. Strange how he and BBW had a somewhat similar experience. Of course he didn't bed down the squirrel. As for Shelley Lee Wilcox – it just figures. The one BBW couldn't have was the only one he wanted to keep.

What words of wisdom would Clara have on the subject?

The waitress slapped the check down in front of Russell.

"About these bills that are mounting up."

"All my money is back there in my suitcase."

"What do you mean? You left cash in the room?"

"Suitcase locked. Money locked inside. You think I'm dumb or somethin'? I spent most of my life on the road, Sonny. I'd never leave cash lying around the dresser."

That's twice he's called me *Sonny*, Russell remembering the police officer's reaction when he addressed him as *Son*.

"If it's not too pushy on my part, Mr. Wilcox, do you mind telling me how much cash is in that suitcase?"

BBW dabbed at his mouth with a napkin. "Forty."

"Forty dollars?"

"Ha! Ha ha ha! Forty thousand. Brand new bills."

CHAPTER 23

Just a Cowgirl

Russell wasn't sure he'd even locked the flimsy wooden motel doors. All that cash in the suitcase. Even locked, anyone around the age of ten could kick those doors in – no sweat.

"I'll have that chocolate layer cake. I want the nice one in the round glass case," Billy was telling the waitress. "That high one." Like she couldn't figure it out? He'd stopped in front of the revolving tower of cakes on their way in looking at it almost hypnotized. Russell had to practically drag him to the booth.

"Now be sure and give me a thick slice with the maraschino cherry on top. Add it on my bill. And a double espresso."

"I'm afraid we don't carry *expresso* here."

Harrumphing his displeasure, he batted an arm. "Just bring me a black coffee. Stroooong."

"Do you still want the cake?" she asked.

"'Course I do! I want the cake and the coffee!"

Russell slid out. "I think we should get moving."

"You go on ahead. I'll come after I'm done with dessert."

"And how do you expect to get there? Hail a cab?"

"I ain't leavin' without dessert."

Russell got back in the booth.

BBW said nothing more until the coffee and cake arrived then he perked up. Russell kept checking his watch. The old man paid no attention. It took him another three quarters of an hour to finish, for Russell to pay the bill and get him back in the car. Trying to move him along any faster was impossible.

Thankfully, the silver hard-sided suitcase was still on the floor by the bed where Billy left it. And still locked.

"Jesus." Russell wiped off sweat beading along his hairline.

BBW burst into song. "*A cowgirl's just a cowgirl 'til she falls in love...*"

Escaping into his own green room, leaving the connecting door part way open, Russell began to undress. Amazing, he thought. The idea of the suitcase being stolen didn't faze the old guy. Then he remembered all those bowls of pennies he'd rolled into brown wrappers, the hours spent doing it, only to leave them to sit in a shopping bag. Because of that, Maggie had called him *an indefinite man*. A stinking bag full of rolled pennies – like it was a crime that he hadn't gotten around to redeeming them.

The old guy continued to croon his old songs. He could still carry a tune. That pureness of sound, the corny country lyrics, made Russell melancholy. Wanting the past back more than he cared to admit.

Finally the songs ended, and he switched off the lamp, breathing the moldy wood smell, the years of people coming and going. He called out "Good night," to the old man.

He didn't really expect a response and didn't get one.

CHAPTER 24

Way More Scenic

Morning dawned clear and bright. And, freezing. Russell could feel the frigid air seeping through thin green wallboard. He'd slept OK. Around seven he poked his head into the adjoining room but BBW was still tucked in and snoring. He had hoped to get an early start, though even getting up at seven didn't necessarily mean an early departure. The old guy slower than spit sliding down a glue board. Speaking of glue boards, Russell was sure he felt something skip across his hand during the night. *A mouse* crossed his mind, but he'd been too sleepy to turn on the lamp.

Under bad water pressure, he stood inside a formica shower stall, hardly bigger than a phone booth, wondering if BBW would be able to pull it off. Well it wasn't Russell's problem. The old guy could go the whole trip without a shower, he could care less. BBW was the type who made you dislike him at every turn.

While Russell was shaving he heard banging, the old man and his walker appeared at the bathroom door. "I'm out of shavin' cream," said BBW.

"You're out, or you forgot to bring some?"

"Whaddaya have there?"

"It's Rapid Shave."

"I can't use that junk it irritates my face."

"Then use soap," Russell said.

"Soap! Are you nuts?"

He looked at Billy then placed his razor on the sink edge. Nina told him *Play your cards right and you'll get a big tip*. Those freakin' cards.

"Look. Use the Rapid Shave this one time and I'll get you another brand when we're on the road. OK?"

"Can I shave in here? My bathroom's cold."

❧

By some miracle they managed to check out and be on the

road by nine, this time paying with bills from BBW's suitcase stash; at least relieving Russell of that particular worry. The old country singer had brought along very few clothes, it was mostly bills in brown bank bundles taking up the main section of the suitcase.

Since it was along the route they had breakfast in the same diner, only this time they were served by a different waitress. BBW making a few loud comments mentioning the waitress from the night before as being *an extremely beautiful lady*. Russell could see it embarrassed the girl on breakfast duty, who was lumpish, a bad case of rosacea on her face.

"You might try being more sensitive to other people," he said in a low voice. "You've hurt this girl's feelings by saying how foxy the other one was." Frankly, in Russell's opinion the other one wasn't anything to brag about either.

BBW, glaring across the table, dug in hard. "I didn't say foxy. I don't use that word. Don't like it. Never did. A woman's a woman and a fox is a fox. They don't smell the same."

What's the use? thought Russell. The guy is half senile.

After breakfast he put a country music station on in the car. Playing some real hillbilly crap. BBW remarking from the back seat after each song. He liked this one, he didn't like that one. At first, Russell couldn't find any rhyme or reason to his choices. Then a pattern began to emerge. Dolly Parton, who BBW *liked*, was also a singer he'd performed with many times. The ones who'd dissed him, didn't want him sharing their billing, BBW really despised, calling them names. *That Cretin* he'd say, *that Cretin should learn how to sing.*

"Which route we takin?" he asked around lunch time as Russell pushed west through Pennsylvania.

"Well for Colorado this would be considered the southern route."

"I specifically requested the northern route! It's way more scenic and the food's better."

Northern diners are better than southern diners? Russell shook his head. Though why anything coming out of the old man should surprise him... "It's winter, Mr. Wilcox."

"Not yet!"

"OK, it's almost winter." Russell nearly said *winner,* forcing himself to hold back. "We don't want to run into those winter storms."

Illinois, Iowa and Nebraska would be bad enough, before they dropped down into Colorado. Dropped clear off some mountain.

Russell gripped the wheel remembering Clara's warning about mountains. That Clara! Jesus! Even Ohio and Indiana could turn treacherous. It was nearly *winner*, already *winner* weather in some of those states. He chuckled at his little private joke then sobered up quickly. He hadn't considered weather problems when Nina offered him the job. Even taking the so-called southern route. The Lincoln had rear wheel drive. It would slip and slide like the big whale that it was.

Somewhere in mid-Pennsylvania he'd started taking a dislike to the car. On dry pavement he found it way too easy to maneuver, feeling it lacked soul. Tension. He could practically steer the thing with one finger. From the outside, it had begun looking like a hearse. The triple-black, that he first thought was pretty cool, had started feeling tight, confining. Or maybe it was the company he was keeping. He reached for his phone.

"No phonin' while drivin'!"

"I'm just checking my messages."

"Keep your eyes on the road."

He tossed the phone back on the passenger seat. No point in arguing. The old guy never gave up his position. He'd go down yelling, he was one of those. This chewed at Russell, reminded him of the squirrel day. The fact that he had gone down quiet in the street. And not just that terrible day. When Maggie left he'd been quiet. Even in the army. Clara knew. She said he gave up Maggie without a fight. She wasn't even there and yet she knew.

The old guy continued his carryings on about the northern route. "Madison and St. Paul!" he cried out. "Pierre, South Dakota! Now there's some beautiful country. Not like these lousy highways you're takin' me down."

Russell slowed the car, easing onto the shoulder of the road. He parked, took off his seatbelt, turned around and looked BBW square in the face. "If you really want the northern route it's going to add time to the trip. Maybe a lot of time."

"How much?"

"I don't know. I have to map it out all over again. It could cost you a lot more in the end. Maybe a bundle." What would Nina and Leo have to say? He'd been instructed to take the southern route. He assumed Nina had priced the trip accordingly. "The extra time could add significantly to your bill," Russell said. *Am I turning into an accountant*?

"What exactly is your hurry?" said BBW.

What exactly?

CHAPTER 25

Pipe Dream

At lunchtime he phoned Nina who had twenty-seven fits. She screamed. "No fucking way! The Lincoln can't handle it. You've got lakes up there and hundred mile an hour winds. You'll kill the transmission! Then Leo will kill you. Then where will I be?"

Nina had worked the whole thing out to *her* disadvantage.

Typical. Maggie pulled similar stunts. Never mind it was Russell stuck with an old crazy man, and the prospect of blizzards, black ice, sleet, freezing rain. Possibly freezing to death! Did Nina think the southern route was via the Caymans?

He hung up. "Nina said we can't switch the route."

"Dang woman!"

Russell teetered between relief and disappointment. BBW had stirred something in him, something about the northern route. True, he'd never seen South Dakota or Cheyenne, Wyoming. Maybe that was the appeal – see something he'd never given much thought to, then all of a sudden it's an opportunity smack in your face – almost like scaling Everest. It felt exciting. He'd been a *flat ground guy* all his life, bound up in his geography. New Jersey.

Now by comparison the southern route (not exactly *southern*) seemed wrapped up in a cocoon of less severe weather; at least initially. Of course soon the tables would turn. The tables and tides, he thought. Scraping the idea of the northern route as a crazy pipe dream by a crazy man – BBW. Wishing they could go *real southern*, chuck the car, get on some sailboat bound for tranquil waters.

"How'd you like to go to Colorado via Cuba?" he said jokingly.

"The northern route!" screeched the old man from the back seat.

There was nothing Russell could do. Nina had signed off in blood – his blood. *Leo will kill you.* It wouldn't surprise him.

Furious at what he called *total bullshit*, the old man screamed about the route, refused to eat when they stopped for lunch, then just as Russell forked his final hunk of tuna, BBW flagged a waitress and ordered a bear claw and tea.

"Isn't that more a breakfast item?" said Russell.

"I grew up on 'em."

"Where did you grow up? Jersey?"

"The garden stink state? I grew up in South Carolina."

"In that case I'd have thought a more southern route would appeal to you."

"Well you're wrong." But his eyes lit up when the waitress set down the plate with his bear claw. "This is a nice big one," the old man said smacking his lips.

CHAPTER 26

Southern Route

Dusk came on quickly. One moment it was daylight, the next Russell found himself scanning billboards for motels; eventually spotting one for Travelodge 3 miles ahead. He turned off the highway onto a quiet country road following yellow markers pointing (hopefully) in the right direction. What was to stop some local yokel from flipping the signs to read the opposite way? As he was mulling this over, a red truck zoomed past honking and traveling at some insane speed. He was glad to finally see the sign on the motel roof. The idea of traveling in darkness with the old man didn't strike Russell as a great thing. As he pulled into the parking area, BBW began yipping from the back seat: "Can't we at least find a Hyatt for criminy sakes?"

Any answer would be useless.

"I just loved those places with the heated towel rods, when I played the London Palladium. You got up in the morning, took a deep soak then wrapped yourself in a hot towel. Shelley Lee used to love to wrap up in those big white monogram robes at the Park Lane Hotel. She loved them scones, too, with the thick cream." The old man moaned. "What's it all come to? Billy Bud Wilcox stayin' at these kinda places?"

Kenny Rogers, also not to the old man's liking, had been singing a duet on the radio. When the song first started BBW had called them *those two*.

"Shut them off!" he yelled.

"Did you say that hotel with the heated towels was in London?" Russell had never been to London, or anywhere really. Only where the army dumped him.

"Well I said so, didn't I?"

Cranky old dog. What did he have to be mad about? He's been pretty famous and made a lot of money, had all those women and traveled the world. What's his problem?

"You should be grateful for what life has given you," Russell said. Surprised to hear this coming out of his own mouth.

"I'm grateful."

"Then why are you so grouchy all the time?"

"It's my style. Plus I don't feature dyin'. That part's right around the bend."

Russell made the radio louder. Brenda Lee doing an upbeat love song. "We have to stay here, there is no Hyatt," he said.

"She's a little cutie, that Brenda." The old man clicking his teeth. "I coulda had her, but it didn't seem right. She being practically a baby."

He could have had Brenda Lee?

❧

A couple of times during the night his shouting woke Russell. Their rooms were side by side but thankfully not connected. He could hear BBW carrying on behind the wall.

Finally he banged on it. "Mr. Wilcox, are you all right?" When he got no answer, he wondered if the old guy had come to that bend in the road he was so worried about. Laughing to himself, Russell fell back into a deep sleep and didn't wake up again till almost eight-thirty. Now they wouldn't be on the road till eleven. He banged on the wall shouting, "Are you up Mr. Wilcox?"

Putting his coat on top of his pajamas, Russell let himself out of the room. Bright sun hitting his face caused him to slide on the icy outdoor walkway. He grabbed the iron railing. Overnight, the cement had turned to glass. And this is the *southern route*. Russell pounding on the old man's door. He tried the knob, finding it unlocked.

Shaved and dressed BBW was standing there without his walker.

Russell pointed at it near the wall. "Do you think this is a good idea?"

"I feel like a million bucks!"

"You won't if you fall down and break a hip. It's icy. I almost fell, myself, out there."

"You have poor balance. Anyone could see that." He was focused on Russell's arms. Always with the insults.

"Look. Just don't go out by yourself. Do you understand? I have to take a shower. Then I'll come by and get you."

"Hurry up, I want my breakfast."

CHAPTER 27

Autographs

At the Pancake Palace the old man called attention to himself by singing bits from some of his more well known recordings. A few times Russell said *Sshhh*! but it didn't deter BBW. Four older ladies at a nearby table applauded. One getting up and coming over to ask for his autograph. The old man obliged by pushing up her sweater sleeve and signing her arm with a green ink pen she supplied. "Love from Billy Bud Wilcox," the woman gushed reading her arm. When she turned away, he pinched her on the butt.

"Oh, Billy." She was dimpling and giggling.

"What's your name darlin'?"

The old man spreading it on thick, and the ladies loved it. Thicker than I ever could, thought Russell, embarrassed to admit this. And at the same time impressed by the old man's ability to bounce back. Sexy behavior from a man who just yesterday declared his life was bending toward ending.

Meanwhile, Doris, the *signee*, was encouraging the others to have their arms signed.

"I'll write anything you want," said BBW growing louder. He was relishing the attention. He pointed at a silver-blonde with a poodle cut. "And what's your name darlin'?"

"Louise." She sat there smiling.

"I'll sign your cute ass, any day, Louise."

A surge of hysterical laughter rose from the ladies. "Sign mine *Mildred*!" another one said, popping out of the chair to stick her butt practically in his face. "Go on," she said wiggling her ample backside, "I dare ya!"

A dangerous gleam lit up the old man's eyes. Russell pulled the pen away. "I think Mr. Wilcox is done with his autographing for today."

"Says who!" BBW's face contorted. "Who died and made you

king? I'll say when, who and what! Gimmee that pen! Give it to meeeee!" He flailed his arms. "I ain't goin' anywhere till Missy here gets her autograph."

Russell slid a napkin in front of him. "Then write it on this."

BBW grabbed the woman by her hips, shoving his face against her butt, sort of rotating it. "Shelley Lee," he moaned. "What have you gone and done to yourself?"

Russell lunged just as Mildred managed to break away, her table of ladies quiet as a tomb.

"Go Shelley Lee!" he shouted. "Go and don't ever come back!" Hunched in the chair he was sobbing out of control.

Russell squatted next to him. "It's OK, Billy." He patted the old man's knee. "It'll be fine, you'll see."

A big guy in a plaid flannel shirt strode over. "I'm the manager, any problem here?"

Russell shook his head. No problem. What could possibly be wrong? "Come on, Billy," he said helping him up.

CHAPTER 28

A Big State

For a while they traveled in silence with the radio playing the usual country tunes. A Burger King drive-thru took care of lunch, and they continued on.

"Where we at?" the old man asked at some point. He sounded sleepy.

"Still in Pennsylvania."

"It's a big state."

Initially so bright, the morning sun had evaporated into a murk of metallic gray sky. Russell tried making small talk but BBW seemed distracted. A few times he caught him dozing through the rear view mirror, waking up, dozing again. He kept the radio at low volume. Felt kind of sorry for BBW. After his crying jag he looked more like an old bag of bones than ever, the camel hair coat hanging merciless on his gaunt frame. Obviously that Shelley Lee situation did a number on him. "I was never the same," the old man had told him, sniffling, and letting Russell lead him out of the Pancake Palace.

As the two o'clock news came over the radio, he piped up from the back seat. "Tell me about the love of your life." As if none of the morning drama had ever occurred.

"Are you talking to me?" said Russell.

"Who else is in this car? Just you and me. Me and you. Right or wrong?"

"I guess so." Russell feeling uncomfortable. It didn't strike him as the sort of thing he wanted to share with Billy.

"Come on, now. Don't be shy. You saw my crocodile tears. Let's see some a yers."

"You want me to cry?"

The old man chuckled. "Not cry. Bare your soul, boy."

Bare your soul boy. A song he might've sung at the height of his career. Except Russell never bared his soul. Never. Asking Stan if he considered Maggie *nice* was about as far as he ever got baring his soul. He wasn't even sure he had one. If people asked: Do you believe in God? Russell always said: I don't know. No point agreeing to something that felt unimaginable, extreme, even far fetched. The day the squirrel jumped out of the tree, if someone had asked: *Do you believe in God*? He would've said: *I believe in the devil. The devil jumped out of that tree and bit me*. Of course nobody asked.

"Cat got your tongue?"

"What was the question?"

"You gotta ask twice, no point askin'."

Russell groaned. "Do we have to talk about this?"

"Yep. If you want to clear the slate."

Clear the slate! What a joke.

He listened to an ad on the radio for Listerine. He thought about telling the old man how he was walking along minding his own business when this *rodent* (as Clara called it) flies out of a tree – this virtual Batman attacking him on the neck.

"Her name is Maggie and she left me," he said.

"When?"

"Some time ago."

"What season?"

"I don't know. Winter I guess."

"Ah-ha! I knew you had issues with *winner*. You don't like it. Maybe you used to, now you don't. You and Maggie husband and wife?"

Russell groaned again. "Do we have to do this?"

"If you want to get your mind free. Or do you want to be daft in your old age?"

As if you're not? thought Russell. "I feel like having a pepperoni pizza."

The old man cracked up laughing. "That's Maggie talkin' from your gut. She's still got you hot inside. Still smokin' for her. You want to eat her pepperoni, that's what you want." He made obscene noises with his lips.

Dodging a truck that nearly took off the front end of the Lincoln, Russell had to laugh too. One minute the old guy was practically dead, the next he was grabbing women, the next telling his tale of woe, then dousing you with his so-called wisdom. What a handful! No wonder Nina had Leo bow out. She knew Leo would've murdered Billy the first 24 hours. Russell knew, too. Hats off to Nina, he was thinking. On the radio a corny old song *Hats Off To Larry* had just finished playing.

"Sexy?" asked BBW. "Your Maggie, was she sexy?"

Russell cleared the frog in his throat. "Maggie was very attractive in a skinny sort of deranged way. She *was* sexy."

"How skinny? Biafran?"

Biafran. Now there's a word from the dark ages, where BBW dwelled. Russell wondered if Biafra even existed as a country, or had been swallowed up by another nation decades ago?

"Not quite Biafran," he said playing along. "Just skinny. You know, like a girl instead of a woman's body."

As soon as it came out he knew how it sounded. Weird. It wasn't that. He didn't lust after young girls. It's just that he liked women before they got so fully formed they turned into the monster mode feared and despised by most men. Heavy, solid. Built for child bearing and child rearing and little else. Bodies armored with flesh that hid delicate nerve endings. War-like bodies, warring bodies; ready to stand up to men. Fight.

"I have to admit she had a certain delicacy," said Russell. "Her body, that is. Not her mind. Her mind was a steel trap with fangs."

Traffic on the highway was increasing as they got into the rush hour. Hard rain began pelting the car. Russell thought of bullets shattering the windshield. Wondered if he still had some remnants of PTSD leftover from The Gulf? He pictured Maggie poised on the hood pointing a weapon at him. Them. He and Billy. Merged into one indistinguishable form: Men.

"What else went wrong?" said Billy.

"I didn't say anything went wrong. I said she was skinny."

"Wrong again. I'm gonna tell you somethin'. Now listen up. You require a woman with *heft*. Otherwise you find out you're datin' a colt or a calf. Depending."

For a while Russell had been noticing an odd smell in the car. Did he step in something along the way? "Speaking of colts and calves, do you smell something funny?"

"I have a little gas in my tube."

"What do you mean, tube?"

"My super pubic tube. Why do you think it takes me so long to pee? I gotta deal with my bag. Ain't easy. Messy. Didn't you notice?"

CHAPTER 29

Vanity

Traffic was backed up, barely moving. The rain continued coming down hard. Russell could barely make out the faded white lane lines. Billy kept napping on and off.

"So your Maggie is sexy and skinny. What else?" Startling Russell – coming out of nowhere like rising from the dead.

"Billy, I don't know. We just didn't make it." Russell hit the horn at a light-blue Camaro that was weaving, then moved into the center lane. He didn't care to discuss the particulars.

"We just didn't make it," the old man repeated.

"She wasn't big on blow jobs."

"None of 'em! They don't like it. My second wife, Velva, used to screech at the very idea. She said all that stretching made her lips chapped and creased. At breakfast she used to point out a new lip line after each one. *Tuesday's blow job* she'd say, pointing to some line I couldn't even see. It's their vanity. You mess with their vanity they'll hate ya for it."

Russell was sick of the whole conversation. He'd heard enough. Maggie didn't complain or show him lines on her lips. One night she dragged out the suitcases. In between, he'd gone to war and come back.

"You still want that pepperoni pizza?" asked Billy.

Russell shook his head. "No."

The temperature was dropping. He increased the heat, asking Billy if he was cold in the back. Billy said he was *doin' fine* then wanted to know if Russell had any kids.

"The war got in the way."

"What's that got to do with fuckin'?"

CHAPTER 30

The Colonel's Chicken

The sign read *Welcome to Ohio.* Billy saw it and chirped, "Welcome to Ohio. Welcome to Ohio. Welcome to Ohio." Like that mynah bird he lived with back in Jersey.

Russell didn't comment. For miles and miles he'd been thinking about kids. Kids they never had. Sure he'd wanted kids. Lots and lots. A whole football team of boys, a cheerleading squad of girls. So many kids it would take a stadium to house them. He used to want them so bad he started feeling them inside, like he was pregnant and carrying. He read it was a syndrome and some men actually experienced labor pains. When he tried discussing it, tentatively, with Maggie, ashamed about his feelings, she told him to get a grip. She had no interest in being a mother. She wanted a career in interior design doing up rich people's mansions.

On the border of eastern Ohio they stayed at a Quality Inn. Both he and Billy unusually tired. A bucket of *The Colonel's Chicken*, pale biscuits, mashed potatoes and gravy delivered to the room. Because of an air duct convention, they had to share a twin. Beds separated by a night stand and lamp. A white laminate dresser under the window held the other lamp. No frills. Billy, propped up against pillows on his bed, was munching a fried chicken leg.

"Will you take a look at that *pitcher* hangin' near the bathroom. The frame ain't right."

Stirring gravy around in his mashed potatoes, Russell gave it a glance. "A landscape. Yeah, the frame is a bit ornate for the scene. But no big deal."

"No big deal? Everything in here is chained or bolted down. Can't you see what's in front of yer face? It's like we're in *lockdown.*"

"You swear you've never gone to jail?"

Billy got that look in his eye, similar to when Russell thought he might bite Mildred on the ass. "I been inside. Once."

"Now it's your turn to talk!" Russell feeling a momentary spark after days of dull nothingness.

But the old man was dropping off, head lolling; the chicken leg landing beside him on the beige bedspread. Not chained down. All it would leave was a grease mark.

CHAPTER 31

Never-Never Land

Ohio, with its *highways and byways* (as BBW put it) was an interesting enough state to drive through. So far the weather was cooperating. Cold, but dry. Pretty in its rural parts. Russell thought he might come back to Ohio some day when he had more time. On his own. Maybe by then he would have found another woman, even another wife. And together they would travel through Ohio. When he got back to Jersey maybe he'd run into Fig, and they would make a connection and become lovers. He didn't really believe this. When he had stood up, on his own two feet, after the squirrel, he didn't really want her anymore.

Nevertheless, with nothing else to think about, he let Fig roll around his mind; companionably; like being at home smoking a cigarette in a squishy chair. Unlike sitting in a car seat (that belonged to someone else), driving an old man somewhere that felt like never-never land.

The trip was a huge drag. Russell feeling restless and jittery most of the time, while Billy, on the other hand, seemed to have taken on a more relaxed attitude. Becoming accepting of certain things. At least he'd given up on the heated towel rods and what he called *hotel products*. He'd finally stopped ragging Russell about some cream rinse with a French name in a red bottle that he used to *just adore*.

One night after finishing supper, BBW said, "Let's go to a cowboy bar. I saw one a few blocks over while you were stopped at the light. I want to get drunk. How 'bout you?" The old man was grinning. "Take your mind off Maggie."

"My mind is never on Maggie."

BBW burped. "Those beans are killin' my stomach. Too much blackstrap. Nobody knows how to make beans right anymore, you got to bake 'em slow, and easy does it on the molasses. That's the trick pony."

The last few days he hadn't been shaving. His white stubble was thickening into a short beard that made him look even older. And, in Russell's opinion, kind of mean.

"I don't know if I'm up for a cowboy bar," he told Billy.

The old man was wigging over the idea. "Trust me, you'll love it! All those cowboys twirlin' cowgirls on the dance floor! I swear! It'll bring the juice back into your heart."

Again about his heart. What the fuck? First Maggie said it, then Clara with her cards, now Billy wanting to bring the juice back. What juice? And why *his* heart? It's a good heart Russell was thinking, touching himself on the chest. Why does everyone want to tamper with it?

CHAPTER 32

Underground

The cowboy bar sign Billy noticed from the corner turned out to be an underground bar – down a long steep flight of cement steps. Russell thought of the thirteen cement steps leading to his front door, then thought of the squirrel and got a sharp twinge in his neck.

In a cold wind tunnel, between buildings, they stood watching people coming and going. The music rising to street level was loud and tinny. "I don't know how we'll get you down there," Russell said. "I don't see any possibility."

"Do you think it's a live band?"

"I have no idea. Does that make a difference?"

"I kinda wanted a live band."

All Russell wanted was to crash in the room with the TV. Billy, hunched over his walker, looked older tonight. More frail.

"Hey young feller!" BBW gripping the arm of a blond guy who looked in his twenties. Russell couldn't tell ages anymore. Cooped up 24/7 with the old guy, everyone else looked prepubescent.

"You musta heard of Billy Bud Wilcox?"

"You mean the country western singer?" The blond kid was tall and gangly.

"Key-rect!"

"You saying you're Billy Bud Wilcox?"

"Bingo!" The fuzzy white chin lifting with pride.

Before he could rationalize it away, Russell felt a little pride, himself, for knowing this crazy but somewhat famous country singer.

"Peaches. C'mere. Meet Billy." The kid pulling over a gorgeous black girl. "This man is Billy Bud Wilcox the country western singer."

Russell unable to take his eyes off her. What a face and body.

Wishing he could touch the wild black hair bursting curls onto her shoulders.

"Oh," was all she said.

She has no idea thought Russell, looking from the girl to Billy. The old man, of course, was beaming. He had no idea that she had no idea.

"I've heard of you," said another young woman. Not as pretty, but not shabby either. More rangy blond and tall like the guy. Another brother and sister act? Russell studied them. Another Nina and Leo?

"I'm Sonia," said the blond.

Continuing to beam, Billy jerked his head from one girl to the other, like he couldn't get enough, fast enough.

"This is my boyfriend, Tad," said the girl named Peaches.

Russell watched her pull Tad close so that her breasts disappeared into his side. Wishing it was his side she'd snuggled up to.

"Glad to meet you, Billy." Tad stuck out a hand.

"Sonia and Peaches and Tad," said the old man, a lilt to his tone. Repeating it a couple more times, like he might turn it into a song.

Naturally he hadn't introduced Russell. Probably wouldn't have, if Russell didn't speak up. "We were trying to figure out how to get Mr. Wilcox down these stairs."

Now he wanted to be down there as much as Billy wanted to. He wanted to sit in close proximity to Peaches, watching her, watching her dance, maybe. That was sure to be sexy.

"This is my driver," said BBW by way of introduction.

Knock yourself out thought Russell.

The three kids said *Hi* but nothing more. Then Tad said, "We can carry him down the stairs. One on each side." He looked at Russell. "It'll be easy, dude."

Russell narrowed his eyes. Sure, *dude*, why not. At least it would get him down there near Peaches for a while. At least an hour or so.

Both of them hoisting an arm under BBW's armpit, with the long camel coat dragging, they got him down the steps and into the bar. Sonia followed behind with the walker. Peaches came five minutes later, after making a stop in the ladies room. By then they were packed around a table near a wall, Russell making sure to maneuver so he got a chair next to the empty. Tad parking himself on the other side.

Smiling and laughing, Peaches slipped in between them. In the dim smoky bar light she looked even hotter. She took a flask out of her large leather bag, saying, "They don't mind here, as long as you fill from their supply."

"What's that you're drinkin'?" BBW winking, piling on the charm.

"Tequila." She smiled back at him.

"Enough of that will fry your eyebrows."

The three burst out laughing. "You are too much," said Sonia.

"I am?" BBW stared into her face, all phony innocence. "Get me a Jack D," he shot over his shoulder at Russell, winking and blinking at the two girls who honestly seemed to be enjoying him. It's sickening thought Russell; ashamed to have felt a bit of pride just moments ago; deciding BBW was nothing but an old wind bag.

He stood up looking around. The place was jammed. He muscled his way over to the bar, the music so loud his ears started ringing. He saw a woman climb onto a fake bull, its ugly hairy hide lurching and jerking, while all the fake cowboys and cowgirls cheered. She fell off pretty quick. The old man better not get any bull riding ideas. At least he hadn't demanded Russell find him a cowboy hat. Not yet.

CHAPTER 33

Once or Twice

"I've sung with them all," Billy was bragging when Russell returned with the drink. "You name me a legend and I'll have sung with that person."

"Elvis?" asked Sonia.

"Yep, Elvis. I opened for Elvis in Vegas, once or twice."

He opened for Elvis in Vegas once or twice? Russell eyed him skeptically.

The place was hot and getting more packed in. Everyone having a high old time. He circled the table, setting the drink down in front of BBW. It being Elvis you opened for, wouldn't you know if it was once or twice? Russell sure would. Even an ego as big as Billy's would know that. Clara flitted through his mind – what would she have to say about this Elvis business? Then he thought about Maggie, skeptical of anything she couldn't pin down. Slipping into the chair next to Peaches, he forgot about everything else.

CHAPTER 34

Ranch

It turned out they were all twenty-three years old.

"Well, now, ain't that unusual." BBW slinging the country hash worse than ever. Still not a single one had asked Russell his name. If anyone got around to it, he was going to say: My name? My name is Driver. Like Minnie. Only backwards. It would probably go clear over their heads. They're just kids, he was thinking. Kids live in a different world.

"That we're all 23 is really not all that unusual," Peaches was explaining, "because we grew up together on the same street, and we went to the same grade school, then junior high, then high school."

"Fascinatin'." BBW stared into her eyes.

Russell watched her reach up to brush the front of Tad's hair. "You had a little tiny leaf stuck," she said.

It made Russell shiver, like he was the one being touched. He was picturing her body under the tight jeans and yellow T-shirt. Was her bush (BBW's word) the same untamed curly black as her hair? Peaches. Delectable. Peaches, he decided, was one of those tame on the outside, un-tame on the inside, un-tame on the outside kind of girls. That type could be very confusing but were seldom dull.

Tad, in his Mr. Cool role, seemed bored; like he didn't notice her touch him. Right! And BBW sure noticed. The old rheumy eyes perking up.

"Y'all should come with us," he was saying.

"What? What is this?" Russell sat straighter in the chair. The music was blasting out Loretta Lynn. Maybe he misheard. "What did you say?" he asked the old man who was pointedly ignoring him.

"You folks want another round?" A cowgirl waitress dressed to match the décor.

"Sure, darlin', drinks all around," said Billy. Then telling the three kids they'd be *more than welcome* at his ranch in Colorado. The first Russell heard of any *ranch*! In the car he distinctly heard BBW refer to his place as a big white house on its own cul de sac. Now he was pimping the place as a ranch!

"It would be something different to do," said Sonia. Playing with her satiny blue-gray scarf, sliding it back and forth along her neck. It looked like an eel in his opinion. But the kids were getting psyched as Billy talked up the ranch and all the fun they'd have in Colorado.

Shit! Russell was thinking. Sure it would be great having Peaches in the car – what man in his right mind wouldn't want Peaches in the car? But it was impossible. Impossible. Nina would stroke out.

"OK, OK, listen up. This can't happen. I was hired to drive Mr. Wilcox, and only Mr. Wilcox. Capeesh?" That was Nina's word. If it took capeesh to set them straight he was happy to borrow it.

"Fuck off," said BBW.

"What!"

The old man pounded the table. "You heard me, I want the kids. They're comin'. Nothin' you can do about it. Nothin'. I want the kids to spend Thanksgivin' and Christmas at the ranch."

Russell groaned. The ranch again! Tempted to say: It's only a house on a cul de sac. That mundane detail might put an end to things. A ranch. They probably expect horses all over the place. Plus he didn't even know if it was legal for him to have other passengers in Leo's car.

"Mr. Wilcox, this is not going to happen," Russell said.

"You're fired!" Waving his arms, BBW nearly knocked over a stumpy orange candle.

Tad stood up quickly. "See what's happening! You almost started a fire, Russell."

The old man was shouting unintelligibly, his mouth sunk like quivering liver in the white whiskers. He blurted out, "Tad can drive us!"

"You can't fire me because you didn't hire me. Nina did." He looked around the table at the kids. "I'm sorry, I'd like to be able to take you along but it's out of the question."

Peaches put her hand on top of Russell's. "Who'd know?" She tilted her head, gazing at him from under thick, curly black lashes.

He felt himself tremble, start to turn hard, unable to move his hand away. He knew he should. Get it away. It had been a long time. A woman's heat. All that. Peaches' hand continued to press down. Tops again, he thought, Maggie careening through his mind. Maggie preferred tops. Pushing her aside (where she belonged) he pondered Peaches' sexual preferences.

"You're done for." BBW was beaming. "Hooray! We're all headed to Colorado for the holidays! Me and my kids. Bless my soul."

I am so fucked, Russell thought. Registering the silk of her hand as it slid off his.

A plan was set. He would pick them up in the morning. Some apartment building a few blocks from the cowboy bar. Sonia wrote the address inside a matchbook. You don't have to do this, Russell told himself, shoving the matchbook in his pocket. Get Billy into the car and just take off. Sure he'd steam up like crazy at first, throw a big roaring fit, but eventually he'd calm down. Though about that last part, Russell wasn't so sure. BBW wanted the kids badly, like a starving man. Certain they'd fill the hole in his belly. And what about mine? he thought. What's gonna fill mine up?

CHAPTER 35

Dangerous

He didn't sleep well. At some point he dreamt about Billy – the old man slicing two parallel lines across the throat of a wailing infant. What that could possibly mean, he had no idea.

Around seven he got out of bed and phoned Stan. "I'm in deep do-do."

"I was wondering how things were going. Haven't heard from you in a couple of days."

Was Stan chastising him for not phoning more often? Then Russell told himself *relax*. Too much time with the old guy, way too much time. It was starting to corrode his brain cells.

"Things not going so good, huh?" Stan was saying. "He still busting your chops?"

"Every minute." Russell peered through the window blinds. Another dismal day. A square light fixture high up on the motel sign had been smashed out. "But it's not just that. He's picked up three people, three kids he wants to bring along. It's a nightmare, Stan. I don't even know if it's legal for me to drive them. I don't know what to do."

"Take it easy, bro, you sound on the verge."

"I am. I am on the verge. If I say no, he probably won't tip me at the end, and Nina said he could tip really big. I've been through hell so far on this trip. A living hell. If I come back without that tip money, I don't know. He's got about forty grand in a suitcase."

Stan whistled. "Who carries forty grand around in a suitcase? In cash?"

"All cash."

"In a suitcase?"

"Well I said so, didn't I? I said in a suitcase!"

"Sounds risky."

"It's all risky. The car is risky, the weather, now these fucking kids he wants to bring along."

"Is it a Samsonite?" said Stan.

"It's one of those silver hard sided jobs with the clamps instead of a zipper." What did that matter?

"They're the latest."

"Yeah? Anyway, now he wants me to take these kids, feeding them a load of crap about this ranch he's got. It's just a house on a private cul de sac."

"That could be nice," said Stan. "With the mountains in the background."

Russell felt cold, climbing back under the blankets. His toes were frozen. He wiggled them to get his circulation moving. "I don't know if there's any mountains near his house. It's not important." He bashed the pillow trying to make a comfortable dent.

"This one girl, Peaches – oh my god, Stan, she's just beyond belief. She's young. Twenty three."

"Peaches, huh?"

"Yeah, and she's hot. Very."

He could hear Stan clearing his throat. "This is a tough call."

"I know, I know it is, which is why I phoned you."

"Well do you think she's going to do you? Sometime on the trip? Is that what's motivating you? 'Cause this could be dangerous."

"Yeah it could be very dangerous! Nina would put me in jail if she found out. And her brother, this crazy guy Leo, it's his car and he'd come after me, Stan, he's the type to carry a weapon. At least a tire iron."

He could hear Stan blowing out air. "It's a quandary."

For a while they went in circles; then Russell said, "I have to rouse the old asshole. Did I mention he has a super pubic tube?"

"You mean one of those catheter pee tubes?"

"Yup."

"I don't think that's the right word."

"What word?"

"You said super pubic tube."

"I got that from Billy."

"Oh." There was silence on the line.

"Stan you still there?"

"I'm scared shitless that could happen to me."

It could happen to any one of us, thought Russell. Saying goodbye to his brother, he clicked off. Groaning, climbing out of bed, he looked at himself in the mirror over the dresser. Gray. Starting at his temples, where there seemed to be a lot more hair.

Men are supposed to lose hair with aging instead he was turning into a gorilla. He touched carefully with his fingertips. The gray spreading into his tired face. Old. This trip was putting on the mileage, and not just the car. Thankfully he didn't look anywhere near as old as BBW who practically looked embalmed. Checking on him occasionally, through the rear view mirror, he'd be sitting back there stiff as a corpse.

Russell was sorry he ever signed on for this; he should have taken Clara's message seriously. Then he thought of Peaches, how she gave him *that look*. He gripped the sides of the dresser. Wanted to jam his nose in her. He went to the crappy bathroom and jerked off in the shower stall under lukewarm water.

CHAPTER 36

The Kids

Naturally *the kids* weren't close to being ready. Their building seemed to be a multi-family house, old and dilapidated, facing a narrow side street. Tad had answered the door wearing sweats and looking half-asleep. On the crooked front porch Russell stared past him at the two girls sprawled on a couch. The kid was rubbing his eyes, asking, "Where's Billy?"

"Waiting in the car."

"I guess you better come in."

The girls were dressed but Russell didn't notice any suitcases. Maybe they changed their mind. On a sagging, beat-up couch they were drinking mugs of coffee under posters of rock stars looking vicious with their guitars. The place smelling like a storage facility for garbage. Peaches smiled brightly at him. "Hello," he said. In the light of day she still looked scrumptious.

"Listen, I can't leave Billy out there too long. And you aren't close to being ready."

Tad stretched and yawned. "Calm yourself, Pops."

"Excuse me?"

"Be cool."

"I'm very cool." Russell wanted to punch him in the nose.

Tad rocked on his heels. "You don't seem cool."

The kid was testing him. And you're a total asshole, Russell was about to say, when Peaches got off the couch pressing her coffee mug into his hand. There was still some inside, about half full.

"This is your coffee," Russell said. He stared at the rim. Her lips had been on this mug. Did she drink right handed or left? He couldn't ask her.

"I can always get more," said Peaches in her velvet way.

"I can't leave Billy outside very long."

"Bring him in for coffee." Sonia sounded bored. "We're practically ready. We hardly need to bring anything, really, just a few changes of clothes and our make-up." She shook a finger at Tad. "It's you that's holding things up!"

"I can be ready in a second."

"Then do it!"

Russell was starting to get the picture. Tad the baby boy, Peaches the soft-voiced little sister, which left Sonia to be the mother. This is going to be some disaster, he thought.

When they finally got themselves together, clumping their bags and whatnot outside the building, he made his way to the car. BBW slumped in the back seat with his mouth flung open. In that moment Russell thought he died. Possibly a heart attack from sitting so long in the unheated car. Then the kids appeared and the old man woke up making a big fuss over who should sit where. They agreed to alternate each leg of the trip, or every day, or whatever. At some point Russell stopped listening. Drumming the steering wheel with his fingers. He wouldn't mind Peaches next to him up front; *that* he wouldn't mind one little bit.

Everyone finally more or less settled, he pulled away from their building. Tad up front, Billy squeezed between the two girls in the back. Despising Tad, he drove faster than usual, feeling the kind of simmering anger Maggie had been capable of stirring in him.

"Now that won't do," BBW was saying.

For a second Russell thought the old man read his mind.

CHAPTER 37

Tampax

After only a short time driving Russell was even more agitated. Berating himself for caving on this deal.

"You're both so pretty," the old man was saying, "you don't need to argue over who gets to sleep in my bed. I'll take you both together. Me in the middle. A meat sandwich."

The girls found this hilarious, even Tad started laughing. Russell didn't find anything funny about it. He was feeling sweaty on the back of his neck though it was another cold day. Who are these people? They could be convicts on the loose. Anything. They didn't seem to have jobs they were worried about, taking off to Colorado so free-wheeling.

"I have to stop for gas," he said. The tank still more than half full but he needed an excuse to get out of the car, move around a bit, think. Billy might insist on keeping the girls in the back seat the whole trip which meant he'd be stuck with Tad. There wasn't enough air up front for them both.

While the car was being gassed, Russell went into the snack shop and bought two Mounds and a Milkyway. Today's weather more dismal than yesterday. As if he were headed toward a gray and impenetrable vortex. Nearing the car, he saw Tad stick his head out the window. "Russell," the kid yelled, "get some Tampax would you?"

Tampax? What do they think they have here, a delivery boy? Ignoring the whole thing he continued toward the car and climbed behind the wheel.

"Let's get a few things straight. I don't mean to be petty but I'm not buying anyone's Tampax. Or anything else. That includes food and lodging."

"I'm payin'!" shouted BBW. "This trip is on me! The kids get whatever they want. I'll pay. I want my kids to be happy."

Russell stared out the window. Gusts blew the scrawny trees planted in groupings. It did nothing much to make the service station more palatable. He bounced the car keys in his hand. These three had Billy by the balls, the old man lapping it up like a thirsty dog. "Fine. Pay for whatever you want. I don't care. But I'm not getting anyone their Tampax. However, I will wait while you go inside and get it."

"I respect you for that," said Sonia leaning forward and touching his shoulder. He could feel her face close to his. "It was for me, and I told Tad to shut up about it. Why can't you shut up, Tad? You only end up alienating people. Nobody wants to be anyone's slave."

"My ancestors were slaves," said Peaches.

"I'll just be a minute," said Sonia.

Russell watched her walk past the pumps toward the snack shop. She was very tall but had a nice sway, her blond ponytail bobbing. He peeled the wrapper off a Mound watching her disappear into the snack shop.

"What's that chocolate I smell?" said BBW.

"He's eating a Mound," said Tad.

"Who? Who's eatin' a Mound?"

"Russell."

"I want a Mound," said BBW.

Russell went on chewing. Ordinarily he'd pop out of the car like a jack-in-the-box and get the old guy his Mound. Today he didn't feel like it. When he finished, he unwrapped the second one, aware that they were all aware of what he was doing.

"He's got two," said BBW.

"That's plain selfish." Tad pulled out a cigarette.

"Not in here you don't. No smoking in this car." Russell gave him the hard stare till Tad put the cigarette behind his ear. And don't cross me, he thought. None of you better cross me.

Sonia got back in the car, then.

❧

After lunch at Taco Bell nobody switched seats.

"It's so comfy back here," Peaches was saying resting her head on Billy's shoulder.

"You cozy up, sweetheart."

"Back here is fine by me," said Sonia.

BBW looking happy as a pig in shit. Saying *my kids* or *the kids* every other breath. Tad liked the front seat for the extra leg room.

Not if I saw them off while you're sleeping, thought Russell. He gritted his teeth and started the car. "Does anyone need to use the bathroom? If so you better go now."

Tad, who looked high all the time, was making frequent trips to the Mens Room. He claimed he had to pee every time Billy had to; making Russell suspicious. Girls peed a lot; everyone knew that; and old men. Russell hardly had to pee and he would turn fifty in December. He gave Tad a sideways glance. The passenger seat way too close in his opinion. The kid caught Russell looking and grinned like they were best friends.

"You are one upset dude," Tad said.

"Don't fuck with me."

"Hey! Hey! None of that talk! My girls don't like to hear cussin' or swearin'. Right girls?"

A little while later, Russell heard a purring sound coming from behind. He stiffened. *What a bunch of sickos.* He thought about phoning Nina, right then and there, pulling the plug, stopping their joy ride. Get rid of the three of them. But then he'd have to explain why they spent almost an entire day crossing a good part of Ohio in Leo's car. Like Stan said *It was a quandary.*

CHAPTER 38

Kaboom

The old guy had taken on some color in his cheeks and he couldn't stop grinning. About an hour past Cincinnati, Peaches said *Ouch that hurts* and Billy said *I'll try and be more gentle.*

"What's going on back there?"

"Mind your beeswax," the old man said.

Then Russell decided there was no choice but to phone Nina. He cracked his window a few inches – the car feeling close, claustrophobic. What *was* going on back there? Clara's cryptic message came rushing at him – *Proceed with caution.* He decided those words covered a lot of ground, and dropped his speed 20 mph.

"We're practically walking." Tad rapping his knuckles on the dashboard. "Man at this rate we'll never get to the ranch."

"Cut that out," said Russell. "You'll mark up the dashboard." Leo's dashboard.

"I didn't make a mark. I'm just anxious to get to the ranch. We'll never get there at this pace." The kid sulked.

You got that right, thought Russell, since there is no ranch to get to. And as soon as we reach the next rest stop I'm dumping the three of you out. "Kaboom!" he shouted, surprising himself.

"Kaboom!" Peaches yelled back. The other two picking it up, then Billy, all of them screaming *kaboom kaboom kaboom kaboom*, over and over, like some ancient bizarre blood ritual.

"I swear..." BBW was making a high-pitched giggle. Marilyn Monroe again? The girls and Tad laughing uncontrollably. All on account of one stupid word. His stupid word. Russell felt himself slipping again. At least his interest in Peaches was on the wane. She was like that high def TV-combo-sound-system that you wanted badly, kept looking at in the store, dying to own it; then the salesman tells you the price and you have to walk away. Russell passed a car going even slower than they were, and thought of that song from about a hundred years ago – about the *apples, peaches, pumpkin piiiiiie.*

They made a couple more potty stops for BBW and the girls, with Tad tagging along each time. And each time Russell told himself *Now is when the kids have to get pitched.* Yet somehow...

He stopped going inside on the breaks figuring he'd let Tad do the babysitting.

This particular stop was at a Junket's Family Restaurant featuring a huge lobster sign over the door. They were taking a long time in there. As the army used to say: Check out the operation. He approached the white clapboard building with its bright green awnings. That lobster sign. Strange choices for an inland eatery but wasn't everything about this trip strange? He located Billy and his walker at the first urinal.

"Where's Tad?" Suspicious, Russell looked around the brightly lit white tiled Mens Room. "Where is he?"

"In here, dude," the kid called out from a stall.

"What's wrong with the urinals?"

"In England they say u-rine-als," said Billy.

He could hear Tad laughing behind the stall door.

Russell didn't care what they called them in England. Why was Tad using the stall? Was he faking it? Maybe shooting up in there? *Go on,* he was urging the kid. *Do the world a favor and kill yourself.*

Loopy, and grinning, Tad strolled out and washed his hands.

"You forgot to flush," Russell said. Now he had him! He went to the stall door yanking it open expecting to see a clean toilet bowl; instead finding a smelly pile of Tad's undigested lunch.

"Would you flush for me, dude? Sometimes I forget."

"Russell is very good that way," said Billy.

CHAPTER 39

Kindness and Understanding

By four, the afternoon sky had turned a watery purple. He was tired of driving. Still debating about whether to phone Nina. The indecision added to his exhaustion. Plus it was time to scout out a place for the night. By keeping the kids all day and overnight Russell knew he was getting in deeper and deeper. All of them together in a motel. He'd have to report this to Nina. After going berserk, and Leo going berserk, she'd grill him endlessly and god knows what? Nina could be a professional interrogator, a torturer. He saw how those people operated in the army. Nina was a natural.

Meanwhile Billy was entertaining the kids by telling them how Russell picked the worst places to stay. And that he, Billy Bud Wilcox, preferred to sleep in the *lap of luxury*. And all he'd slept in so far on this trip were a bunch of *flea bags*. The kids laughed harder. They seemed to laugh at everything the old man had to say. Peaches laughed most, then Tad, with Sonia joining in towards the end. Sonia was the most quiet. She seemed fairly smart. While Peaches only acted dumb. She was quite smart in her own way, and still incredibly beautiful in Russell's opinion. She wore a perfume that smelled like fresh lemons. Not that it mattered.

"Look, Billy, I don't know if we can keep *the kids* overnight." He stressed the kids like the three weren't in the car. He figured by depersonalizing things, it might bring Billy to what little sense was left in his brain. Fat chance. It riled Billy up.

"I told you...!"

"Yeah, I know what you said, but I've been thinking things over and it just doesn't seem like a good idea."

"Hey, dude." Tad had turned in the passenger seat to face Russell. "You must've boogied around the country in a VW van during The Summer of Love. That was around your time period, right? You must've dropped your share of acid. Some peyote. Had your chicks. Right?"

Russell jerked the wheel hard swinging the Lincoln into the right lane. "You have no idea what you're talking about. How'd you like to get booted out of this car?"

"You're not the boss!" shouted BBW.

"Tad, shut up! Just shut uuuuup!" Sonia yelled.

"Please don't talk to my boyfriend in that tone," said Peaches.

"He doesn't learn!"

"Nobody learns by force. Look what happened when they used force on the black people. We fought back. Everybody got hurt. You have to use kindness and understanding. If you want to make real change."

"That's my sweet little girl," said Billy. "That's my Shelley Lee."

Russell got even more jittery.

CHAPTER 40

A Few Bedbugs

Near the Indiana border, in falling snow, they stopped for the night at one of those places called MOTEL on a peeling sign. Billy was livid. They ate dinner in the MOTEL dining room, the food uniformly greasy. In the morning everyone woke up with bedbug bites. Russell had some on his back and ankles. They itched like hell. At breakfast in the MOTEL dining room, the girls were extremely upset; Sonia in particular. Saying she'd never seen *anything quite like this*; and if this was going to be *the natural state of things*, she wasn't prepared to continue on the trip.

Russell poured syrup over his pancakes. A few bedbugs, he thought, might save me yet.

They were surprisingly tasty and fluffy. "You should make a decision here and now," he told them with his mouth full. He had started to relax. "I can certainly understand you not wanting to continue," he said chewing. This he directed at Sonia, who, after the bedbug attack, was now his strongest ally.

BBW smacked his palms together. "We'll ditch the car and fly to the ranch. I've had enough of these dumps."

The girls and Tim got very excited, everyone agreeing it was a great idea and how it would get them to the ranch in a matter of hours.

A waitress came over with refills on the coffee.

"Just a second." Russell pointing a finger at Billy. "I was told you never fly. Never. For personal reasons. That was the whole point of my driving you to Colorado in the first place. Am I right?"

"Well I ain't skeered anymore. Now that I got my kids around me."

His kids. Three blood-suckers scraping every cent they could out of the old man.

"Billy you are so awesome." Peaches snuggling her arm through his.

Russell put down his fork. "So you want me to drive you to the airport? Is that what you want? I can't fly to Colorado with you. I'll drop you off at the airport and drive the car back to Jersey."

In a way, it was a huge relief. Just dump Billy and his kids, and take a scram: the long, slow peaceful ride home. Alone. It sounded like heaven.

Sonia looked up from her coffee. "New Jersey? Is that where you started Russell?"

He nodded signaling the waitress to come back with the coffee pot.

"Hey, Peach," she said, "Russell is going back to New Jersey. That's pretty close to New York City I would imagine."

Peaches' mouth dropped open, her bright dark eyes widening. "Is that true, Russell?"

Why do you want to know? His own eyes darting back and forth between the two girls.

"Mister do you want the coffee or not?" said the waitress looking annoyed.

"Yes, I'm sorry," said Russell, "half a cup please."

She was grumbling about having to come back twice and now only half a cup. She poured it sloppy, some splashing in his saucer.

"Hey, dude, you live close to the Big Apple?"

"Do you Russell?" said Peaches.

"Yep. Just forty minutes from the city."

"No! No!" Sputtering and spitting, BBW's eyes were bugged out and bloodshot. "We're all goin' to the ranch, it's been decided!"

In her practiced way Peaches drawled, "We been just dyin' to get to New York City." Looking all starry-eyed at Russell and sort of shaking off the old man who was tugging on her sweater sleeve, begging her, and starting to turn teary.

He moaned. "What about the raaaanch?"

Tad belched. "We can do that another time."

"What other time? I ain't got that much time, I'm runnin' short." Billy started sobbing, the way he carried on that morning with Mildred and the ladies.

"Oh, dear," said Peaches. "This isn't good."

"Of course it's not good!" Russell snapped. "It hasn't been good since you three stepped in the car! For you this is some big lark. Meanwhile I've got a job to do. He's my responsibility. I've been hired to drive him home, and that's Colorado. Not drive you to Jersey."

"Well." Sonia pursed her lips. "You've certainly told us."

Russell nodded and finished off his half a cup in one gulp. Let them all go jump. Come hell or high water (certain he'd find both before this was over), he was determined to drive Billy to Colorado. Right to his front door. Then he'd ask to use the bathroom, collect his tip and be on his way. That was the plan. In his mind he could hear Maggie congratulating him. *Now that's decisive* he heard her say.

CHAPTER 41

Lethal

"So far Indiana sucks. Nothing here 'cept fields and dust. Where's the corn? You still awake, dude?" Tad poked Russell on the arm.

He flinched. "Don't ever touch me while I'm driving! And that white stuff on the ground that you call dust happens to be snow. The real deal. Not like what you shove up your nose." Or pump in your veins.

The kid started laughing. "It's funny how things change. Suck is our word but *drag* was the hot word for your generation, right?"

He had gotten in the habit of mostly ignoring anything Tad had to say. Sick to death of him. Buying dope laced with some lethal substance and giving it to him as a present crossed Russell's mind. Guys did that in the army when they really hated someone's guts. *Here, this one's on me,* he remembered one soldier telling another. He pictured Tad getting really high then keeling over and going out slow.

They were coming up to a red barn, half up and half down. "I could let you off there," Russell said. You could go there to die.

Tad just laughed his giggly goon sound. "The Wizard of Oz blew the roof off."

The Wizard of Oz. Jesus! Here he was feuding with a kid half his age. Sobering. This is what the army does to you, thought Russell. The army, plus one old crazy man and three insano kids. Turns you into a killer. He never felt much like a killer during his tour in The Gulf. He felt scared, and bored sometimes, and sometimes lonely for Maggie, who hardly answered his letters. That should have been a red flag; but Russell was too busy worrying about being blown up.

"How many more states before Colorado?" Tad wanted to know.

When Russell didn't answer, Sonia said, "How many more?"

It was becoming *a thing*. Because he usually ignored Tad, one of the girls would pick up the question, repeat it, forcing a response out of Russell. It started with Peaches but now Sonia was in on the act. In the overall scheme, Sonia at least showed some class. Her tall, lean body had started looking sexy to him. *Stick thin but hot* was how he described her to Stan over the phone. Her breasts all nipple through the tight T-shirts. Her flat breasts and narrow hips and tight ass were getting to him. Stan had said, "I like that body type, too, good for holding on."

Today Sonia had fixed her light hair into a single braid down her back. He found it an intelligent and neat way of wearing your hair. When he fantasized about Sonia, intelligence came into the mix. Her hair would stay put during sex. While Peaches' hair, that seemed to be everywhere at once, would get caught in your eyes, your mouth, shoved up your nose, shoved everywhere. Up your ass if you found yourself in that enviable position. He groaned inwardly. Peaches' hair was impossible to deny.

❧

The hours passed slowly in the car. Tad, slumped in the other seat just inches away, making his dumb remarks, fiddling constantly with the radio, dicking around with Billy and the girls. While Russell was doing his best to keep the car steady despite snow, a lot of it now, and ice and other distractions. Such as Tad's legs crossing and uncrossing every few minutes, the full red mouth flung open while he napped, the dragon breath. *Try Scope*, thought Russell.

And hour after hour, Russell got more and more horny due to the close proximity of the girls. They had no modesty. At night they flitted in and out of Billy's room, through the connecting door, half-dressed. Victoria Secret push-up bras, sheer camisoles, thongs so small why bother? This morning Sonia had strolled into his bathroom stark naked asking to borrow some toothpaste.

Toweled around the waist, Russell had been shaving. When he saw her like that he cut himself on the cheek. She'd come up close, hadn't showered and her smell was all around her. He kept his one arm locked tight against his side, hardly moving a muscle, at the same time using the other to try and stop the bleeding. All the while hoping Sonia would make a pass at him. She took the toothpaste tube off the sink saying *Thank you.* Adding: *That's a lot of blood for such a light scrape, do you have a clotting problem*?

Strange, this Sonia.

Passing a truck on the wrong side (no one in the car even noticed), again he thought: Strange this Sonia. Like the squirrel, who *had* dug deep, yet drew no blood. Or, so it's been said.

CHAPTER 42

Town Without Pity

When Russell chose a route that bypassed Indianapolis entirely, the kids had lots to say. Billy, too, naturally taking up their cause, doing plenty of bitching and moaning.

"Indianapolis is a great town," the old man was saying. "What a pity! A pity we ain't gonna get there. I played Indianapolis so many times. More times than you got toes and fingers." From the back seat Peaches started gasping and giggling like she was being tickled. "All of yers combined," he said.

Uh-huh, thought Russell. "Indianapolis," he said, "is a town without pity."

"I know that song, it stank," the old man countered.

Lately every exchange with Billy was like playing poker.

They stopped for lunch in a town built around the turn of the century. That other century, thought Russell exiting the car and shaking out his stiff arms and legs – suddenly feeling a hundred years old himself. The girls were excited over the quaintness of the place; plus *all the cute little boutiques* squealed Peaches. "They must have amazing antique jewelry here." She swung her wild black hair. Snow dust falling from a pine tree frosted her curls.

Clinging to his walker Billy lit up like a firefly. "I'll buy you a ring! You too, Sonia, darlin'."

With Billy's walker setting the pace (making crawling seem fast) the kids moved toward the Giraffe Café, a narrow, purple Victorian house set off by a bright-yellow front porch. Ankle deep in snow, glad he'd packed his father's boots at the last minute, Russell stood next to the car.

"Aren't you coming?" Sonia called back.

"In a minute."

He leaned against the fender phoning Stan. "It's a nightmare."

"You still have those kids?"

He couldn't answer.

"Bro, what's going on? Can you hear me?"

"I hear you. I'm about to cave. Billy keeps passing out the cash like Monopoly money, right now he's going to buy them antique rings. He'll run short at this rate. The girls are naked half the time. That idiot Tad is never not stoned."

It wasn't entirely true; he'd only seen Sonia naked, and just the one time.

"It's really boring here," said Stan. "It keeps raining and Mom is driving me nuts with her hypochondria. Clara's driving me nuts, too. Your trip sounds like a party."

Clara? "What's Clara up to?"

"Oh, you know, that spooky stuff she leaves on my machine, those warnings. Come to think of it, she left one the other day for you."

Clara left him a warning? "Well, tell me!"

Stan cleared his throat. "Damned if I can remember."

"I'm in snow up to my yin yang. I'm miserable. Try! Try!"

"OK, take it easy! I think it had to do with water. Yeah, yeah. Something... about water. A water fall, I think."

"What?" Russell wanted to shake it out of him.

"I think she said like Niagara." Stan laughed. "See, I remembered! I'm not senile yet!"

"Niagara?"

"She said for you to keep your eyes open at Niagara Falls."

Russell stood there taking in the old midwestern town, its narrow crooked houses with gingerbread trim, the line of antique streetlights. "She's nuts. Plain nuts. Niagara Falls is upstate New York and Canada! Does she think I'm headed for Canada? Maybe she mixed up Colorado for Canada. You said she gets stuff scrambled on the phone."

Stan let out a groan. "I don't know what that woman thinks. Any of 'em. Women are a mystery. You know that show Unsolved Mysteries? They should re-name it Unsolved Women. That would be a pisser, right?"

The snow was coming down harder, the black car losing itself under a veil of white. The way I'm losing myself, he thought, feeling the snow hitting the brim of his Knicks hat. Sorry he'd phoned his brother. He felt very distant from Stan; like they'd passed in the night and forgot they had a blood bond. He wanted to ask whether Stan still thought of him as a brother, deciding against it. Stan hadn't done anything specific. Still. Everything seemed out of proportion. A bird with a giant wing span circled overhead making a cawing noise. Expecting the worst, Russell ducked. The massive creature had moved on.

CHAPTER 43

This is America

"We were playin' a game," the old man told Russell. "You coulda played too, but you stayed outside and snubbed us."

In the Giraffe Café the four were squeezed around a table. Billy looked mean, cantankerous, edging for a fight. His white beard, grown longer, didn't help soften the old features.

"I had to make a phone call." Russell sat at the next table. The Giraffe Café had a warm smell like bread baking. Dotted curtains. Small pine shelves with knick knacks. Comforting. He wanted to rest his head on the round marble table but knew that would show weakness. They were waiting – to dive in and make a meal out of him. "I see how you saved a chair for me," he said.

The old man screwed up his face. "Who'd you call? That Nina woman?"

Does that worry you? thought Russell. He watched them watching him. "As a matter of fact, I phoned my brother. Stanley."

"Where's he live?"

Why this sudden interest in his family? Russell picked up a purple menu in the shape of a tulip. "He lives in Jersey, too, not far from your place."

"Bet he'd like to live in my place! Ha!" BBW winking at the kids. "My place went condo and now it costs a small fortune to buy in. Like my ranch. Cost me a small fortune, too. But I'm lucky. Made my dough while I was still young enough to enjoy myself."

It all sounds too fabulous, thought Russell. The waitress, a middle aged woman with thinning hair in front, was hovering. "I'll have egg salad on toast. With mayo and lettuce. And coffee with Half & Half," he told her.

"Half & Half?" The old man had screwed up his face.

"Would you like to start with soup?" asked the waitress. "Split pea is the special today."

"Nobody told *me* about split pea," said Billy.

"Sir, I definitely mentioned it when I took your orders."

"No ya didn't."

Russell felt his neck getting tight. "All right, Billy. If you want the soup you can still have it."

"Not now. It's all backwards. Everything slippin' backwards. Just like with Shelley Lee."

"Here we go again," Tad said.

The waitress stood there waiting.

"No soup," said Russell.

But by then BBW had gotten sidetracked by the girls, who were yakking about the vintage jewelry he was going to buy them once they finished lunch. Tad, shoveling in a second bowl of purple ice cream, looked up to say, "The house special for dessert."

"I love my kids," Billy was saying. "My kids all have healthy appetites. They follow the healthy approach to life."

Russell could hardly keep a straight face.

When he finished his sandwich and coffee he vetoed their jewelry outing, saying it would take up too much time. They booed him. BBW spewed obscenities. Why don't you all just throw tomatoes, thought Russell.

Everyone in a huff, they left the café. Drove an hour or so longer with the snow coming down thick. Russell decided to call it quits for the day.

"See, it turns out there was lots of time to get my ring. And one for Sonia." Peaches tone sounded accusatory.

In the long run you'll thank me, thought Russell; but he didn't really believe it.

❧

The days ticked by. Lousy snow weather, the highways and back roads, strip malls and the little towns. He continued to circumnavigate the cities. So this is America, thought Russell; while from the mouths of BBW and his kids came stupidity, mostly; selfish stuff he tried blocking out. Nina had left a few messages on Russell's cell, her last one a direct order that he return her call or else.

Hard to control on the ice, he felt the big Lincoln as a behemoth whale under him, slipping and doing its strange dance, all blubber and no traction. Every so often he thought of Clara's warning: Niagara Falls. Even Clara couldn't be that clueless, even she would have some sense of direction. Why this strange *misdirect*? Good old Clara. Russell telling himself *everything's relative.* Even her floppy hat which he'd begun to think on with a certain affection. He'll phone her, clear up this Niagara confusion. It felt like a decade passed since that day she read the cards . As for the squirrel – that felt like a lifetime out of focus.

They should have reached Colorado long before now. Under normal circumstances (Russell taking some deep breaths while stuck in the slow lane), under normal circumstances Billy would already be home and he'd be on his way back to Jersey. Whistling a happy tune.

CHAPTER 44

All the Rage

On a scrubby back road detour, they passed a tepee with large signs out front advertising discounted cigarettes, moccasins, beaded junk. Peaches, still determined to have her ring, whined as they drove by. Then Tad yelled *Look a totem pole*! managing to get Billy all worked up.

"That totem must be 40 feet high!" Billy shouted, and Tad said, "We could strap it to the roof of the car," and Billy said, "That would look mighty pretty at the ranch."

"Please go back Russell." Peaches using her most syrupy begging voice.

Reluctant, he circled back. "Hey," he said, "we could strap Tad to the roof of the car and put the pole up front here."

Nobody was paying attention. They were far too excited about the many wonders they were certain to discover in the tepee.

The moment the girls stepped in past the flap their shopping radar kicked in hard. Ignoring a swivel rack of postcards and cheap key rings, they went straight for the locked case, where they tried on every sterling silver necklace studded with turquoise, all the earrings, bracelets, and rings. Even Tad began to pace complaining it was taking too long. The tepee had a dry funny smell. Somewhere between mildew and overly sweet pipe tobacco. The dark interior making it extra chilly. Russell sat down on the only stool. Then he got right up offering it to Billy. But the old man, reveling in his machismo, refused to sit, saying he needed to be up close and personal when his girls got their bling.

"Bling?"

Tad bent over chortling. "Dude, you are so not with it."

A pudgy woman behind the counter, chain-smoking unfiltered cigarettes, started hee-hawing. Whenever she had to take something else from the case, she clamped down on the cigarette between flat yellow teeth. Kind of nauseating, thought Russell.

The tepee smell, her teeth, the whole freaking scene. Even Billy didn't make a play for her.

"You sure you don't want to sit down?" Russell asked him again.

"I ain't tired." After about twenty minutes more of jewelry insanity he started looking chalky.

The girls, meanwhile, twirled in front of the mirror, moving this way and that in murky light.

"You tried on everything that ain't nailed down," said Tad. "I'm waitin' in the car."

The kid was beginning to talk like Billy. Russell watched him stride out not quite closing the flap all the way, feeling a stream of cold air blowing in.

"You pick, I can't decide." Peaches looking worshipfully at Billy. She seemed about to burst from happiness, swaying her wrist as several ornate silver necklaces dangled. Personally, Russell didn't find anything special about them. He thought it all looked like cheap hooker jewelry.

"I can't make my mind up, either, they're all so gorgeous," said Sonia fingering the necklace she was wearing.

"Get 'em all." Hunched over his walker Billy sounded out of breath. "Get all them necklaces and be done with it." He swayed. Russell jumped off the stool just as Tad strolled back inside, saying, "What about me? What do I get?"

Russell moved Billy, protesting the whole time, onto the stool. Then he stood over the girls. "Choose, and let's get out of here."

Billy didn't scream or argue. "Tad get the suitcase," was all he said.

"Me, again!"

"Go," Russell told him, "and make it quick."

Tad brought the suitcase from the car. Russell counted the money for their loot which totaled four hundred and seventy five dollars. He shook his head. "I can't believe Indian baubles could cost this much."

"Native American," said Sonia arching an eyebrow. "Native American turquoise silver has become very sought after."

"It's all the rage." The proprietor licking her nicotine-stained finger recounting Billy's cash.

CHAPTER 45

X

The snow seemed to be tracking them – Russell felt like a deer pursued by a white hunter determined not to quit. And the slow going got even slower. Not to mention Billy's tube and bag requiring frequent stops. The girls and *their* bathroom stops. "Can't you people get this coordinated!" he said. Delays. Endless delays.

Somewhere, in some state, he had lost all desire for Peaches. She basically just annoyed him now. Billy kept her next to him in the car, next to him when they ate, walked, just about everywhere except the Mens Room. The old man even took to sleeping on the floor beside her bed (she shared with Tad while Sonia had the other bed). BBW slept curled on a bathmat on the floor like a dog.

When Russell found out he threw a fit saying Billy would catch pneumonia for sure and they'd never make Colorado. It fell on deaf ears. That night he was back down there on the mat. Russell gave up. Sleep wherever you want, he thought.

As for Sonia's naked bathroom appearance, he wrote it off as something that that generation just did. X Rated.

❧

Huddled around the bar of a Holiday Inn somewhere outside Springfield, with snow falling quietly beyond the double glass doors, Tad suggested a game of strip poker.

"We don't have any cards," Russell said quickly, figuring that would put an end to it. Besides, he'd seen the girls naked or near naked so many times it no longer sparked his interest.

"Strip poker," repeated the skinny bartender. Up till then he'd been silent pushing beers across the bar. Younger than Russell by at least a decade, the guy was balding and flounder white like he never got any fresh air. Tad and the girls had already consumed their *healthy share*, as Billy liked saying, and everyone was in a high old mood. Billy taking swigs of bourbon out of Peaches' personal flask. Gross, thought Russell who felt forced to stay sober under the circumstances. He'd quit after two beers.

"I believe I can help you out," the bartender said. Reaching under and producing a fresh pack of cards. "If there's anything else..."

"No!" Russell said in a loud voice. "Cards will be fine."

The girls exchanged looks. Tad yawning. "Russell is such a drag," he said.

"I told ya he's a drag," said BBW. "He never wants to have any fun."

Every day that camel hair coat seemed bigger. He rarely took it off now, complaining he was cold without it. Maybe he really could feel his time running out, thought Russell. Maybe the body had an internal mechanism something like a clock, and the old man could feel its winding parts running slower than usual. Who knows?

As for the clock that's running this trip – that piece of shit must have a lifetime battery. Russell swirling the pinch of beer that remained in his bottle.

Good bye, he would say to them all when the time came. Good bye, and fare thee well.

CHAPTER 46

Hardening

Without a word Russell stood up and left the bar. In order to reach his room on the second floor balcony it was necessary to go outdoors and climb an open stairwell. Nobody had shoveled the stairs or balconies. The snow, cold and wet and chilling his face, felt soft and powdery underfoot. Almost lovely. As he walked he counted the doors of the rooms. He had this strong sensation of wanting to lie down out there.

He thought of his house, his fish, Fig, the squirrel, Clara, and his brother Stan. Not necessarily in that order. He thought of the roosters strutting on his kitchen wall. Even the squirrel had become less of an enemy. When he was outdoors, most of the time he hardly gave trees or squirrels a glance. Shaking off all this sentimentality Russell thought *I'm hardening*. Walking a straight line to his room.

CHAPTER 47

Food Groups

Stan sounded reluctant to give out Clara's number. He kept changing the subject, first asking Russell about the girls, and had anyone turned up nude again, then he asked about Billy, then how the car was handling in the snow.

"I'm not exactly going to hit on Clara, if that's what's worrying you Stan. I am about a million miles away, or did you forget?"

"Look. She said she doesn't want to talk direct to you. She'll help you, but only through me. She said she'll operate like a *medium*. Those are Clara's distinct wishes."

I've got a few distinct wishes of my own! thought Russell; but nobody seems to notice or care.

"I can't go back and forth between you and Clara. It's too time consuming. Stan I'll go insane. I've got the old man and these stinking kids on my back, and it's snowing all the time."

"What state you in?"

"Illinois."

"Chicago?"

"No way! Are you kidding? The kids want me to stop in every major city but I refuse. They'll take off with Billy, do weird stuff, and I'll never find them. Him! It'll slow me down for days. They're a strange bunch. I asked what kind of work they do and not one person mentioned having any kind of job. Can you believe it!"

"Actually, yes." He could hear Stan chuckling. "Before you took on this gig, bro, you were kind of in the same boat. For a long time as I recall."

"Don't compare me to those looney birds! I was in the war, how can you even..." Russell began to pace the small area at the foot of the bed.

"Take it easy, take it easy. I was just trying to make a simple point that Clara made the other day."

Russell stood at attention, felt his ears prickling. "What point?"

"She said that we, meaning people, are basically all alike, that there's only about five different groups and everyone fits into one group or another. She said to think of it like the basic food groups."

"Food groups! That's the most fucked up thing yet to come out of Clara."

Stan groaned. "See, this is why she won't talk to you. She says you're blocked. She says you block on every truth. She says it's frustrating to talk to you because you keep looking every direction but the one you're headed."

"She said all that?" He sat on the edge of the bed.

"I swear to God."

Russell sat looking out the window, white flakes dropping through an inky sky. After a moment he jumped to his feet.

"That's crap! She thinks I'm headed for Niagara Falls! She's the one got her direction scrambled, not me. I know where I'm going. Colorado."

"You sure about that?"

"Ah, fuck. You're messing with my head."

"You sound different, bro."

"I am different. You try doing this and see how different you become. Don't fuck with my head."

"Why would I do that, you're my brother."

His brother. Russell felt a stab to the chest, took a breath and thought he might start to cry. He waited it out.

"It's confusing all the time. Jumbled. These kids, Billy, the car. They've got it all jammed up with this shit they keep buying. Billy bought them these really expensive necklaces. Like movie stars wear. The trip is taking forever. I even slashed my face shaving, the day Sonia walked in naked."

"Sonia is the tall blond?"

"Yeah. She's not that bad."

Stan laughed. "Especially naked."

Russell felt darkness behind his eyes. Disjointed. Was he going down? But his brother kept laughing and he finally joined in. "I just want to get this over with and get home."

"I'm telling you, it's really boring here."

"You wouldn't want to trade places, Stan."

"Maybe not."

CHAPTER 48

Snake

Russell came last to breakfast, the table a wreck of foods, the kids and Billy hysterical over their game of strip poker. BBW had stripped down to his underwear and tube, the girls to bras and panties, Tad to his socks, the skinny bartender to nothing.

"That guy's got a snake tattoo near his privates," said Billy. "Imagine that!"

"That's to make his short dick look longer," said Tad.

The girls were laughing uncontrollably.

Very interesting thought Russell stifling a yawn. He ordered oatmeal and coffee, looking around the room. Large and sunny, it could be any of a million motel breakfast rooms in this country. When the oatmeal came it was gummy. He pushed his spoon through the lumps, adding more and more Half & Half.

When Peaches said, "Billy I love you harder than ever," Russell put down his spoon and stared at her. *Now what's going on*? The old man's pointy tongue darting in and out of his lips.

Later, when they were jamming more crap into the trunk, he saw BBW slip Peaches a wad of cash.

"What about me?" said Tad.

"I'll have no bickerin' amongst my kids. You'll each get yers in turn."

"They got those necklaces, too." Tad sounded whiney. But then he poked Billy tickling him, and the old man shrieked and Tad grinned showing deep red gums. Inflamed gums. What kind of dope inflames the mouth? That snake tattoo coming into Russell's mind again. One that ingests small animals while slithering along the forest floor. When Tad brushed past him to get in the car, again Russell saw a snake: this time tightly wound around a tree trunk.

CHAPTER 49

Bypass

With the days growing shorter, darkness seemed to fall in a matter of hours. They were hardly on the road when it was time to stop for the night. The snows continued. Thick and powdery, fine like silt, mixed with ice and freezing rain, the snows continued. In some motel bed, somewhere, Russell dreamt of salivating bloodhounds on his heels; while deep inside he felt a growing loss of sensation: in that one day was the same as the next. The nights, the breakfasts, lunches, dinners. The talk. The bullshit. All echoes in a stone cavern.

He was starting to feel like a slab: stepped on, spit on, written on, shit on, snowed on, his fingers aching from clutching the wheel as he tried keeping the car on a steady path –while as a man he floundered – the kids getting the upper hand at every opportunity; manipulating Billy with their every wish and whim. Sonia included.

Russell decided she stank. Not just her body that he could often smell in the crowded over-heated car; picking out her odor distinctly. Unwashed, Sonia smelled too ripe and a little sour. Smell was how certain animals picked out their mate in a pack of thousands. Take the penguins. He'd seen it on the Discovery Channel. Well one thing was for sure: Sonia would never be his mate. Her classy, intelligent airs were an act. Fake. No way did he want her anymore. Or, Peaches. He wanted to get to Colorado then get the hell out.

He thought of changing the route the way pilots change altitude when there's turbulence. Maybe he should swing further south into Missouri, go through Kansas then across to Colorado. Maybe it would bypass some of this snow.

CHAPTER 50

Crooked From The Outside

At another grimy roadside diner they stopped for lunch. Crooked. Like its foundation was sinking. "I'll be in shortly, start without me," Russell told them. As if they wouldn't anyway.

"Watcha doin', callin' yer girlie friend Nina?"

Every day Billy was more and more hillbilly. He drawled every other word. The girls loved it. Peaches saying it reminded her of *back home.* A short while ago Russell might have picked up the bait, asking where *home* was. Not now.

"I have to check something," he said.

When he took out the map, he didn't want them around, their two-cents worth, complaints about the hick towns, how he took away their fun by deliberately keeping them out of the big cities. You got that right, thought Russell – your *fun* is the last thing on my mind.

He noticed a family of five leaving the crooked diner, each carrying a doggie-bag. They looked content, a nice family who must've enjoyed their meal. No bickering. No angling to get something more out of someone. He couldn't name a single meal he enjoyed this entire trip. As for Nina, she hadn't phoned in the last 24 hours. She probably figures they fell off a cliff. Just as well, he thought, with no intention of phoning her. One more person bitching at him, for sure he'd drive off the first mountain range. He chuckled imagining the nervous breakdown Leo must be having over the car.

Technically he could just disappear. People did it every day. Mommy goes off to the supermarket and never returns, no she never returns; leaving hubby and kiddies behind. The newspapers portraying *the leaver* as a saint: She just went out to buy a box of cake mix for little Sally's birthday party and hasn't been seen in a week/month/year. Casting the *one left behind* in the role of axe-murderer, psychopath, serial rapist. What a world, thought Russell, rubbing two day's worth of face stubble.

In this particular case, the ones left behind would the loonies, crazos, spoiled brats. Billy and his kids. Billy the Kid. BBW seeming more and more fetus-like, shrinking further down inside the big coat.

Russell unlocked the glove compartment taking out the map. Tracing the southern route with his finger, stopping at a jagged line. According to the map key the jagged line represented a mountain range. Switching to the southern route meant he'd have to go clear over those mountains. Russell folded the map and put it away.

❧

Next to Peaches, stuffed into an orange vinyl booth, BBW looked weak, his eyes more blood-shot than normal. Russell pulled a chair over and sat at the table end. He ordered rice pudding, usually safe by diner standards. When the waitress finally brought it, the kids had more or less finished eating and the old man's lids were drooping.

"Rice pudding?" said Tad. "That won't put hair on your chest." It set them off like laughing hyenas.

"Anyone notice this place looks crooked from the outside?" said Russell.

"Looked straight to me," said Tad. Again they burst out laughing. This is funny?

A mom-type waitress, overhearing, confirmed Russell's suspicions. "It's crooked, all right," she said. "They dug around the foundation and down into the cellar looking for grenades hidden in this very spot." She puffed out her ample chest as if proud of her role in the history of the diner.

"Grenades?" Tad sat up straighter.

"Live grenades. German spies hid them during World War Two."

Russell studied her carefully but the woman seemed legit. "That's quite a story," he said. Hoping they found all of them. Nothing like sitting down to a mac n cheese only to be blown to bits. In The Gulf, Russell always felt on a tilt. In this generic diner he actually was on a tilt. Here in the good old U.S. of A.

The kids, quickly bored by the story, were pushing at each other and laughing. Tad fell sideways out of the booth. It hit Russell. "You're all stoned." They turned quiet. He stared at Billy. "Billy, too. You got Billy high. Look at him. What did you give him? He's an old, sick man. Are you crazy or what?"

"I can handle my p-p-p-poison," said Billy, making the kids crack up all over again.

"Not if you want to live long enough to make it home."

The old man made no response. Sat like a stoned Buddah, his coat a mess of food stains. While Billy shrank his ears seemed to have grown. Peaches had been trimming his ear and nose hairs at night, and giving him manicures when his nails started to curl into what Billy called my Howard Hughes stage. Theirs' was a strange relationship. Russell tried not thinking about it; because when he did it gave him the creeps.

"If anyone slips him anymore shit, anything at all, even an aspirin, all three of you are fucked. You got that?"

Surprisingly, the girls looked ashamed. Sonia saying, "You're right. Sorry." Peaches kept her eyes down and focused on her empty plate. Tad was too stoned to do anything but look stoned.

"You could've killed him," said Russell. "How'd you like to have that on your conscience?" Not to mention your criminal record, he was thinking. Certain that Tad, at least, had a record. Maybe even the girls who looked like they could turn shoplifting into an art form.

"Nobody's killin' no one!" BBW's hands flapped weakly then dropped in his lap. He looked terrible. Puffy-eyed, exhausted. Swallowed up by dirty camel hair.

Russell got out of the chair. "Something has to change here. And, fast." He'd lost his appetite for the pie a la mode he ordered after the rice pudding. I'm eating too much sugar, he thought. "We're going to switch in the car," he told them. Bust up your little ring of trouble.

Tad was saying, "Does that mean I get to drive?"

"What?" Peaches shot Tad a look.

"It means you get to sit in the back," Russell said. "One of the girls will switch with you, I don't care who."

He despised them all, uniformly; no distinct differences. In his opinion all of them were losers. Mean spirited, too. Who would feed drugs to a half-dead old man?

He helped BBW out of the booth. He was hardly able to stand. Things had sunk to a new low. Russell felt furious in a way he couldn't articulate. Billy, usually quick to refuse help, went along willingly. He didn't hit Russell or scream when he buttoned the coat to the top. He didn't demand to finish his cherry pie and melting ice cream. An indifferent bag of bones, he could barely cling to the walker.

In some town, in some motel room, somewhere – Peaches had decorated Billy's walker by winding strips of colored tape: crime-scene yellow, orange, electric blue, chartreuse, red, and black stripes hid the metal frame. Tad calling it *Billy and his amazing Technicolor walker.*

The girls picking up on it, too. Chanting that slogan as Billy pushed along relishing the attention, gripping the multi-colored monstrosity and grinning and waving like he was on the Red Carpet, every time they went into a café or coffee shop or bar or motel lobby. Russell found the whole scene revolting. They'd turned him into a side-show freak. Frankly, with or without its decoration, Russell couldn't stand the sight of it. It skeeved him. In back of his mind was the worry – someday I might be chained to one.

Now Billy clung on, hardly able to walk, his head dropped forward.

"Move it!" Russell ordered the rest of them as he steered BBW toward the exit. Tad calling out, "Technically, nobody paid the check."

CHAPTER 51

His Amazing Technicolor

As he started the engine, Sonia slid into the front seat. Snow was still falling but with less intensity. Russell glanced at her. Then backing out of the parking space, he imagined Leo in the rear-view mirror, his teeth jagged and pointy, about to wage an attack. *Squirrel teeth* he thought growing tight across his shoulders. What was Clara's last message via Stan? Hell if he could remember. She can't keep things simple, she can't keep things in a straight line. Making tracks he tore past the gas pumps down a ramp onto the highway.

"Russell's on fire," Tad was saying.

"It feels colder," said Sonia wrapping her long scarf a few times around her neck.

"So what's the plan?" Tad yelled into Russell's ear.

Startled, he jerked the wheel, the car going into a spin, his mind grappling with which way to turn? Into the spin or away from it??? Unable to remember, somehow he managed to get the car back on track.

"Whoa!" said Tad.

"Don't ever mess with the driver! Are you crazy? It's icy and dangerous out here! I don't know what's wrong with you! I'm starting to think..."

"Don't worry." Sonia patted Russell gently on the arm. "We're all in this together."

That, in its own way, almost too terrifying to ponder. Worse than the army. At least the army had trained soldiers at your side. Look what he had. Unable to answer, Russell managed a nod.

Time dragged. Plastic containers of different foods filled the car with a nauseating odor. If he drove at more than a crawl, the Lincoln fish-tailed. He thought seriously about phoning Nina.

Unloading the whole sordid tale. The kids, the car, the weather, the whole nine yards. Kind of like going to a priest. A sort of confession, he thought. At this rate they wouldn't make Colorado till spring. If they were lucky. Russell did not feel lucky.

Meanwhile, in the back, BBW sat quiet as a rock. It wasn't helping to lighten Russell's mood. Normally the old man chattered practically non-stop, working the kids like an audience with his stupid one-liners.

"I'm kind of a little worried about Billy," said Peaches when they pulled into a rest area. Just bathrooms in a cement shed, no snack shop. The parking area jammed with cars and tractor trailers. Russell had to drive a ways past the rest rooms before he could find a parking spot.

He turned in the seat. Billy still looked stoned. But, something else. An expression, maybe. Something Russell couldn't put his finger on. "What's the matter, Billy? Are you feeling sick?"

"Not sick," he said.

"Billy." Peaches stroked his hair back from his forehead. "What's wrong? Don't you feel good?"

"I feel good."

"You don't *look good*, dude!"

"Tad will you just shut-up!"

"Sonia, I'm sick of you telling my boyfriend off."

"Your boyfriend needs telling off!"

"Not by you!"

"OK, both of you shut-up!" said Russell. "You, too!" He pointed a finger at Tad. "We've got a situation here." He realized he was talking *army*. "Billy, do you feel the need to go to a hospital?"

"I'll die here in Shelley Lee's bed."

"He thinks he's with Shelley Lee!" Peaches looked frightened. She pulled on the strings of her hoodie hiding most of her face.

"He always makes believe you're Shelley Lee, there's nothing new about that," said Russell; thinking where have *you* been? Answering for himself: in Billy's wallet. All three of 'em. So busy figuring out ways to fleece him, they didn't even notice what was going on with him. Or, care.

"You gave him drugs he can't handle and now we've got a big problem." Russell stared out the window.

As these places go, it was a nice enough rest area. Bushy white pines and a long ridge that dropped down into one of those valley towns. It looked peaceful there, everything scaled down in miniature. If Billy had been OK, they could've spent a little outdoor time stretching their legs and enjoying the view.

"Just walk him around," said Sonia. "He needs to move around in the fresh air and he'll be fine."

"In case you haven't noticed he doesn't walk!" Russell could hardly believe his ears. "How can he push the walker in his condition? He'll slip on the ice and break a leg. Maybe both. Then what?" Then what?

"We can all help to hold him up," said Tad.

"Exactly." And Sonia stepped out of the car.

About to protest, Russell figured what the hell. "All right, then, everybody out. Except you Billy." If the old man heard, he showed no sign of it.

The four of them stood out there. Tad hitched up his pants. "Now what?"

Peaches bent to check on Billy. She whimpered. "He looks crumpled."

"Tad get his walker from the trunk." Pointing, Russell made it a direct order.

"Billy and his amazing..."

"Shut-up, Tad, and get the damn walker," Sonia said.

CHAPTER 52

Prematurely

They managed to dislodge BBW from the car, Russell and Tad each taking an arm to support his body, with Sonia from behind, sort of wrapped around Billy's torso keeping him upright. Peaches stood by useless and weepy. "This is all our fault," she kept saying.

"You bet." Russell was dry eyed, angry. Thanks to these rotten kids, the old guy could be on his way out. Prematurely. But most of all Russell blamed himself. Right from the get-go he should have refused to take them along, letting Billy yelp and carry on all the way to Colorado. Instead, he took the path of least resistance. Maggie used to rag him about that.

They dragged Billy, dead weight, his head flopped forward. His eyes kept closing. Peaches wailed begging him not to die. "His coat is getting all wet." The girl was crying and wringing her hands. Dragged through snow the bottom part had darkened, turning the camel color into a muddy brown.

"That's the least of his problems," said Russell. *Your problems.* Picturing the old man dead, the kids under arrest. Would that make him an accessory? To manslaughter? Murder, even? You never knew how a jury might rule. Besides, ignorance was no excuse for the law – isn't that the way it went down?

"Come on, Billy." Russell was actually praying.

They dragged him around another few minutes. For an old boney man he weighed a lot. They must be heavy bones, thought Russell, when miraculously BBW started getting some color in his face. Tad noticed too. "Billy's come back to life!"

"Sssshh!!!" Russell looking to see if they were being watched. But people trudged toward the bathrooms or cleaned snow off their cars and trucks. Nobody paid any attention.

He took a few gulps of cold air. "I think he's going to be OK. No thanks to you three idiots."

"Billy we're so very sorry." Peaches had dropped to her knees in the snow, hugging his legs about to kiss the old man's feet.

"All right, get up, get up," Russell said. He had no patience left for histrionics. "Let's take him back to the car. I don't need him catching a chill."

Crying harder, Peaches stood up shaking. "Don't blame me and Sonia." She turned toward Tad.

"Yeah, make me your scrape goat."

"It's *scapegoat*. And you're a jerk," said Sonia.

This time Peaches let it slide.

CHAPTER 53

Billy Almost

At least BBW was alive, and freely expressing his sexual hallucinations once again. It's almost refreshing, thought Russell, reminding himself to be grateful for small favors. Billy alive was actually one of those huge favors, the kind Russell hadn't experienced in some time. Billy alive was pretty huge. For all of them.

Since the *Billy almost* incident, things turned slightly for the better. The kids had sobered up; or if they were still getting high it was at night and out of Russell's way. They'd picked up the habit of saying: *that day Billy almost croaked*. Or *Billy almost bit the dust*. Touching, thought Russell. They also seemed slightly less involved in getting money out of him, though he was still operating the suitcase like a trust fund, doling out the green when someone mentioned a sweater in a shop window, a handbag, or some piece of crap. Russell yelling that the car was already past jammed. It landed on deaf ears. Plastic bags under their feet, they were sitting on bags of clothes. The trunk had reached its limit. When they started putting things on the back window ledge, Russell blew. "You're blocking my visibility! One more bag comes into this car, out you all go."

"You got the side mirrors, dude."

"I need to see out the back window."

"Race car drivers never rely on the back window."

"I'm not a race car driver." Russell wasn't even sure race cars came with back windows. Not that he cared. Now they were doing things his way. "And that means no drugs!" he reminded them frequently.

Over that, Tad had had a minor collapse. "I can't operate without a little buzz."

"Then sleep the whole trip. Or better yet take Trailways home. That goes for everyone else."

"You can count on us to cooperate," Sonia said. "Me and Peach."

Since the *Billy almost* incident the girls seemed to get closer.

That night they crashed at the first motel along the route, another miraculous moment: *REGENCY BY THE SEA*. A sparkling white brick building. The sign, painted deep marine blue, crested with a gold wave like a crown over *REGENCY*.

Peaches cooed. "Look, Billy! Tonight you're going to sleep in the lap of luxury."

"I'd rather sleep in your lap, Shelley Lee."

The kids laughed; though a bit nervously. Their general hilarity had cooled down some. Russell wondered why *the sea* in this landlocked midwestern town? By far the best place yet along the route.

Inside the room Peaches was complimenting Sonia on a scarf she was trying out in the dresser mirror: threading the long red silk through the belt loops of her tight jeans then tying the ends in a floppy bow. Billy clapping then shouting out, "Paris!" like he was a contestant on Jeopardy. A scarf he had paid for somewhere down the line. They were all flopped in the old man's room, the one Russell insisted he now use singularly. "No more sleeping on the floor!" he'd admonished Billy.

The kids and Billy were sprawled across the two queen beds. Russell sat in the only chair. On check-in Billy insisting on two queens. When Russell said: *It's only you, why not one queen bed?* Billy had a ready answer: *The other is a snoring bed.* Adding that his snoring was keeping Shelley Lee awake at night.

Russell scratched at his neck. Since the bed bugs he never felt really clean. "What state did you get that scarf?" he asked Sonia.

"She picked it out in Illinois," said BBW. Propped against the pillows he looked totally recovered, and a little pompous; a sultan surveying his harem.

Sonia twirled in the mirror.

"It's her Illinois red scarf," the old man went on. "The rest of her life, whenever she puts on that red scarf, she'll think of Billy Bud Wilcox and her time spent with him in Illinois. Right, Sonia darlin'?"

"That's right, Billy."

He did seem one hundred percent fine. Yet Russell found it strange how the old man had recently started referring to himself as *he*, or *him*, like he'd stepped outside his body and was watching the goings on.

Bored with the kids' antics, Russell returned to his own room. He checked his cell. Nina was phoning compulsively, leaving messages sounding on the verge of suicide. Somehow she'd tracked down Stan, waiting for him on Russell's front steps. Stan sounded squirmy, telling Russell she must've come by every day, for god knows how long, waiting to nab him, when he stopped by to feed the fish. Stan said he almost didn't see her, being that he only came in through the back way. Nina was waving and shouting so loud on the front steps, Stan said, who could possibly miss her? And, of course he told her nothing. Only that he, too, had not heard from Russell. Not a peep. And that she shouldn't worry since Russell was a highly decorated soldier in the United States Armed Forces serving in The Gulf.

At that point Stan said she got very agitated, calling the Gulf War a *big phony oil war*. Adding: *Nothing good about Russell counts.* Stan asked her what the war had to do with Russell's character. Nina said *everything*. That only a really clueless person would think it was safe to be in the Army Reserves.

Clueless, eh? thought Russell.

After her tirade, Stan said she got really pink in the cheeks and he felt like humping her.

"What!"

Then he coughed a bunch of times into the phone, saying he didn't feel it was right for Russell to leave her hanging.

Russell was certain they had fucked. Maybe in his house, even his bed.

CHAPTER 54

Trust

No one could stop complaining.

"This is the longest trip of my life," BBW was saying from the back seat.

"The longest trip in the world," said Tad.

"It's endless," said Peaches cuddled next to Billy with Tad on the old man's other side.

"I can't stand much more of this snow," Tad was saying. "I'm ready to lose my mind."

"About that..." Russell let it trail off. He despised the kid but going there would be a mean sucker punch. He glanced at Sonia next to him up front. "What about you? Don't you have something negative to add?"

"I'm perfectly content." And she smiled what he had come to think of as her *basic blond smile*; bland and inscrutable. Though pretty. In her tall lean way, Sonia was very pretty.

"Sonia's Born Again, dude. They're more mellow than the rest of us. At least on the surface. Me, I'm Presbyterian. I ain't mellow unless I'm wasted."

"We've noticed," said Russell.

The kid was passing around a giant bucket of popcorn that he picked up after breakfast from the movie theatre down the street.

"Watch you don't spill any," Russell said.

Down the street from the Hollyhock B&B where they'd spent the night, an old-time movie theatre was playing *The Rocky Horror Picture Show* 'round the clock. This morning, tattooed kids with piercings, and stiff pointed hair dyed every color, lining up for the show, had blocked the walkway out of the B&B. It was Billy's magic moment. He told as many as possible who he was. Most seemed uninterested. Russell had to push him along to the car or Billy would've stayed all day. It felt like a hundred years ago Russell saw that movie, shocking at the time with its weird bold nakedness. Afraid of coming across like a nerd, afterward he said it was *really great*; like everyone else was saying. Billy claimed to have seen it, too. Naturally with Shelley Lee.

"Don't give Billy any more popcorn, it's making him cough," said Russell.

The old man had been doing a lot of hacking. Maybe it wasn't just the popcorn. "Billy, how do you feel?"

"Never better."

He did seem fine but the constant cough was getting on everyone's nerves. Tad was saying, "I can't hear myself think."

"Who died and made you King?" said Billy.

The kids laughed, every joke out of Billy they cracked up. Russell groaned: Not that tired King bit again. He'd heard it over and over. "It's irritating to your throat all this popcorn. Too salty."

"Kiss my buck-eye ass."

"Dammit Billy! Why do you always have to turn mean?"

"It's his style," said Peaches.

"Why do you always have to come to his rescue? What are you, a girl lifeguard?" Russell was sick of hearing her stick up for him.

"I love him," she answered simply.

She loved him. His eyes shot toward the rearview mirror. She looked placid enough yet glowing. The old man better not have his hands anywhere but his lap, thought Russell. His mind drifting a moment to the southern route via The Caymans. A joke he had shared with Billy before...

"She used to wub me," said Tad, his mouth full of popcorn.

"I never wubbed you, I just put up with you."

Again Russell's eyes jumped to the mirror but Peaches had slipped out of sight. He adjusted it and still couldn't get her.

"All heads in full view!" Kind of like *all hands on deck*. The kids forced it. He had to crack the whip or they'd run him in circles chasing his tail.

"I was just getting something off the floor." Peaches sounding out of breath.

"I want to be able to see everyone at all times."

"You expect a terrorist attack against the car? Is that what's worrying you, dude? You worry too much. Way, way too much. It's not good for your health."

"I keep tellin' him," said Billy.

"What happened with your arms, they get wounded in the war? Partially amputated? They look kind of stumped," said Tad. "Stumpy."

"Tree stumps," said Billy.

Russell leaned on the gas passing a semi that was doing at least eighty five.

"Whoa, dude, we're flying now!"

"Pedal to the metal!" yelled BBW.

Yeah. Not too bad for a guy with stumpy arms, thought Russell. He should be used to it. Guys ragged him all his life. In basic, some fuck-face sergeant said he was surprised the army had *taken him with those.* Russell was holding his weapon, and thought of pointing it square between the sergeant's beady eyes. He didn't like being reminded of his *special problem.* After Maggie said that, he never forgot. Or forgave her. After that he pretty much stopped having sex with her. Went off to serve in The Gulf, and the rest... well...

"Men can be so inconsiderate of other men," Sonia was saying.

A flicker of respect for this tall, pale girl moved through him. But only a flicker. He trusted none of them. Who did he trust?

CHAPTER 55

Werewolves

It wasn't so bad with Sonia up front. They stopped for lunch and he hustled them along so he could be near Sonia again. He fantasized it was the two of them driving to some bright destination. Russell envisioning the place as having water that looked light-purple, with a swirling volcanic center warmed by the sun. An hallucination – the warmth. Cold creeping into the car no matter how high he turned up the blower.

Several times, when Sonia laughed, she touched his arm. Sonia's arms were long and thin inside the pale-green ski jacket. Arms that fit the contours of the rest of her. He thought about her body. The way it looked, and smelled, that morning – in some state – when she showed up naked in his bathroom.

God almighty, he was thinking, wanting to stop the car and run into the woods and jerk off.

"I've had *my* share of insults," said Sonia from out of nowhere.

Surprised, he glanced over at her. "Who would insult a lovely looking girl like you?"

A barrage of laughter rang out. Mostly from Tad who was mocking and mimicking, with Billy jumping in to raise the stakes.

"Sonia is lovely like a werewolf," said BBW, breaking into hysterical laughter.

She twisted in the seat lunging at him. "And I'm going to drink your blood!"

"That's Dracula," said Tad.

"What do you think Dracula is, you dumb freak? Dracula is a werewolf from Transylvania. Where you belong, Tad. In a crypt, a tomb, burned, or frozen under the ground." Sonia sat back in the seat brushing her palms together, like Tad was dust to be rid of.

"Is a werewolf the same as a vampire?" said Peaches. Nobody answered.

Russell had to admit there was a certain fascination to Sonia. She played along with the others, took Billy's money; then when least expected she seemed to have a change of heart. Kind of like the squirrel. Just going along its way, then seemed to have a change of heart. Clara could eat your heart off a plate. And, Maggie too. And of course Nina. Nina was a natural born killer. Stan better watch his ass.

"Nobody loves me like my Shelley Lee," BBW sang out.

CHAPTER 56

Sorry

That night they stayed in what Billy called *my first flophouse.* And that night Russell had Sonia. He hadn't planned it, was just going along, then the knock on his door.

"Are you busy?" she whispered.

The walls of the Stony Monk Inn looked like corrugated cardboard. He whispered back. "Come in."

She still had on the green ski jacket and jeans, plus something long and colorful looped through her single braid. From Indonesia, she told him later. No underwear. That hair thing was all she left on. It kept getting caught in Russell's mouth.

Afterward, rocking her, rubbing his nose across her flat breasts and hard nipples, moving his lips along her thighs and concave belly – when he asked would she stay the night, Sonia said *sorry.*

His bed turning cold again.

CHAPTER 57

Iowa

At breakfast Tad came up with a plan to move the trip along. Everyone was down and already eating except Sonia. Even Billy was on time for a change and not complaining too drastically. He'd said worse things about better motels. A buffet had been set up in the basement, a tight area sectioned off by particle board. Behind it, a boiler could be heard chugging.

"You can't really plan because of the weather," Russell tried explaining.

He was feeling grim when he should be feeling great. He felt like a one-night-stand. *Because you are*, he told himself, struggling to slice through bacon that hadn't been cooked thoroughly.

Tad tapped the water glass with his spoon. "No, you cannot change the weather. But you can change the weatherman."

What's this *twerp* got on his mind? Swallowing a piece of rubbery bacon Russell felt queasy. He covered the plate of bacon and eggs with his napkin.

"Rest in peace," said BBW.

"Amen," said Sonia coming around the particle board. "An underground breakfast. How retro."

Russell shrugged. "I suppose. If you like that sort of thing."

Smiling, Sonia kept at it. "Very 'seventies."

He was feeling tongue-tied and kind of stupid. What is it about beautiful women always getting the upper hand? He added more sugar to his coffee though it was sweet enough.

Continuing to smile, Sonia slipped into the seat between Peaches and Tad; now always left empty. Peaches making a point of sitting away from Tad and next to Billy at every turn.

He noticed Sonia had some color in her pale cheeks. Maybe she did enjoy herself, and would come back tonight for more. He'd almost forgotten how good it felt inside a woman. The hot squeezing protection of those soft walls.

He remembered Stan once saying all women were the Trojan Horse which was how they came up with the name for those condoms. Pretty clever, Stan said at the time. Russell remembered distinctly. Women's inscrutable bodies – like a game of Chinese checkers. Move this way, she comes; this way, she doesn't. Sonia came quick. The second time, too, when he Frenched her. Stan said after *that* they always come running back. Maggie didn't.

"As usual nobody is listening to my idea," Tad was saying.

"I'm listenin', Shelley Lee."

"Whoa! Now he thinks *I'm* Shelley Lee!"

"We're all Shelley Lee," said Sonia. "One way or another."

"Is anyone going to listen?"

Tad's brilliant idea was simple: they should postpone the trip.

"Put down here for the winter," said the kid. "This looks like a good enough place to wait it out. It's pretty nice with all these snow fields. I bet we could even find some work. That's if Billy's money runs out."

"Never!" BBW pounded the table. "I'm a bottomless pit."

"He's not," said Russell. "Not at the rate you three are spending it."

Billy clapped his hands. "I'm gonna get Shelley Lee a pair of earrings from Tiffany. With those rubies and diamonds. Rubies in the snow."

Rubies in the snow. It sounded familiar. Cherry-vanilla ice cream? Russell wondered how old Sonia was the first time some guy broke her cherry?

Peaches looked up from stirring her Corn Flakes into mush. "It's not a bad idea. It does seem nice here, and the people in Iowa are so friendly. That lady in the drugstore yesterday wanted to do my make-up. She said she could make me up to look like a star. But there wasn't time." She frowned. "That's the trouble with this trip, just go go go. We don't even get to stop on Sunday."

"Even on The Sabbath," said Billy. "Go go go."

I don't remember holding a gun to anyone's head, thought Russell. They make it sound like a kidnapping. If anyone's been kidnapped...

"We're going as planned. Me and Billy, that is." Cautiously glancing at Sonia. Buttering an English Muffin she didn't look up or seem in any way interested.

The owner of the place, a thin, frazzled-looking woman clumped down the basement stairs with coffee refills. She wasn't particularly friendly; as if she couldn't wait for them to leave so she could clean up. The woman seemed the right age (unlike Sonia) for a man Russell's age. But he found her totally unappealing. Once, long ago, she may have been attractive, but now she was tight and hard-looking, the life sucked out of her. Nina was hard-looking, too, but somehow managed to make it a little sexy. Apparently Stan agreed. Russell felt his stomach lurch, and couldn't entirely blame the undercooked bacon.

Tad stood up and squeezed around the particle board partition approaching the woman. "What would a monthly rate be to stay here?"

Her thin penciled eyebrows shot up. "You want to spend a month here?"

"You don't change the sheets after each customer," BBW called out.

"I change them daily, Mister." She fixed him with a stare.

"Mine had cum stains. It was disgustin'."

Everyone turned to look at Russell. "Don't look at me," he said. "I had nothin' to do with Billy's stains." Great. He was so paranoid over Sonia he just said *nothin'*. Too much Billy in his life.

"Don't worry," he told the woman. "We won't be staying."

She didn't say *good*, but he felt it on the tip of her tongue.

CHAPTER 58

Love One Another

From the back seat Peaches oohed and aahhed. "Look at those pretty black and white cows in the field. I really like it here in Iowa, such a cozy feeling. All the pretty farms and the animals, and the little towns. I don't see why we can't stay here a while. Even a few days. I'm sooo tired of driving."

"You can stay here," Russell told her. He was idling the car, waiting for Tad to finish cleaning snow off the rear window. Instead the kid was loading in more junk. One less person minus their duffel and plastic bags would thrill him no end.

"You go, I go," BBW told Peaches.

"She's not *going*, she wants to stay. That's the whole point," said Russell.

Tad stuck his head in the back saying, "I'll stay too. That's if Billy's staying." "You mean if Billy's paying," said Russell.

"Tad, I don't want you to stay," Peaches said.

"Billy doesn't stay, Billy and his money are on their way to Colorado," said Russell.

They didn't even try denying it. Convinced that Billy's money was their money.

"If you get out, you're on your own," Russell added. Sonia he hoped would stick. Sitting next to him up front, he avoided looking her way. "And I'm sick of hearing this. Leave me out of your decision making process, OK? But make it snappy 'cause this vehicle is leaving in three minutes."

"Dude, I can't even take a piss in three minutes!"

Russell released the emergency brake. Nobody made a move, and Tad jumped in as the car started rolling. They pulled away from Billy's first flophouse, down the country road onto another and another. Passing snowy fields, Peaches crying out at each silo, cow herd, horse, barn, fence. A fox running across the road made her weepy.

"You'll have your own special white stallion when we get to the ranch," Billy told her.

"A stallion! Do they run really fast?"

"Like the wind, darlin', they run like the wind on fire."

"The wind on fire." Peaches sounding dreamy.

Dream on, Russell was thinking. He practically laughed out loud.

"'Course, that's when they're not put out for stud," said Billy. "Then they get all silly with the mares, start sniffin' those mare be-hinds, and before ya know it we got more colts than we know what to do with. My ranch has so many animals it could be the Barnum & Bailey Circus."

"Which circus?" said Tad.

"Before your time," said Russell.

"Do you have elephants and tigers?" the kid asked.

"'Course not! It's a ranch!"

"You just said it could be a circus."

"Not lit-rally!" Even BBW sounded exasperated with him.

"Let's leave Billy and his animals alone for the time being." Russell negotiating some deep snow. The last thing he needed was to get stuck on this deserted back road.

Tad leaned forward, his stinky breath hot against Russell's ear. "Why is it you always have to control everything? What is it with you control freaks? We all want to stop here a while. It's a nice spot and you don't even notice. How can you sleep at night?"

"Without drugs or pot, that's how I sleep at night!"

"Here we go," said Billy. "I been waitin' for this. It's the same thing with Shelley Lee. Just when you think everything is all set, *whammo*!"

"We should try and get along, make the best of things," said Sonia.

Technically you don't even belong here, thought Russell, about to answer out of habit. Then he thought of Sonia crawling all over him and clammed up.

"We need to love one another," said Peaches. "Even you, Tad. I'll try and love you again."

"You're supposed to love me!" Billy cried out. "How'd you like to wake up dead, Shelley Lee?"

Uh-oh, thought Russell. Fun was fun, but Billy's *Shelley Lee* fantasy seemed to be taking a bad turn. Even old folks have been known to flip out and murder people. What's to stop Billy from whacking Peaches with a lamp some night while she slept? Though lately, the kinds of places they've been staying, most lamps were bolted to the night tables. Still.

"Billy, you don't mean that!" said Peaches.

"I do! I do!"

Russell slowed the car, pulling next to an old stone wall that looked lopsided. Many large rocks had broken off and fallen to the ground. He kept the engine running. Worried he might not be able to maneuver the car out of this snow drift. Fucking rear wheel drive. Russell sneezed a few times. "Where's that box of tissues?" Someone handed it over from the back seat. He blew his nose and crumpled the tissue, throwing it on the floor.

It felt like an eternity since Jersey. Would he ever see his own home again? This latest out of Billy was troubling. Even though it was directed against Shelley Lee; a woman, who, for all practical purposes no longer existed; as a woman or a man. She's *stone dead* Billy told him early on.

Russell ran his eyes along the stone wall. Beautiful in its crude piling with moss showing on top where the sun had melted some snow away. Green. The moss was the first green living thing in some time. He wanted to get out of the car and touch it, stroke its softness. The moss of a woman's body he was thinking. He wondered what Shelley Lee really looked like – despite what Billy believed and told everyone. Billy seeing Shelley Lee everywhere, now. And danger is danger. Peaches, his usual stand-in for Shelley Lee, did exist. But like Sonia said the other day: *We're all Shelley Lee.* Not exactly comforting.

"We're switching seats." Russell hated moving Sonia to the back, but Sonia was tough and smart. And Billy knew it. Hadn't he called her a vampire? Russell felt pretty sure he wouldn't turn her into Shelley Lee. "Sonia, you and Peaches switch."

"Nooooo!" the old man screamed.

"See. You are a total control freak," Tad was saying.

When nobody made a move, Russell yelled, "Do it!"

Billy started sobbing when Peaches opened the door. "I'm losin' her again!" he cried out. "I'm losin' Shelley-Lee!"

"Do it quickly!" shouted Russell, though more for himself than Billy. I'm losing my Shelley Lee, too, he wanted to tell the old man, as he watched Sonia get out of the car. Once she was out of his jurisdiction (the damn army again!) he knew her interest (if there was any) would fly away like birds going south for the winter. Sonia was a *situational girl.* Took what was handy. Not exactly flattering.

Billy sobbed and he sobbed. Stopping to comment on something or other, then sobbing again.

"It's unbearable," Peaches whispered to Russell. "So much held in pain. The poor man. I hope I'm never in that much pain, I couldn't stand it I don't think."

It was unbearable. It was breaking his ear drums. Russell made the radio louder wondering what Sonia was thinking in the back seat. So far neither she nor Tad had anything to say to the other. Billy seemed to take no notice of them flanking him.

CHAPTER 59

Howard Johnson's

After a quick drive-thru lunch at Dairy Queen (Russell concerned about taking BBW out of the car) they were back on the highway, things relatively quiet, when Billy said, "I'm going to kill you."

Nobody asked who he meant to kill. He fell fast asleep. When it began to turn dark and they were pulling into a Howard Johnson's he started making his wake-up grunts. The tall original green and orange sign was still standing, but a neon roof sign said Peony Motor Inn.

"This used to be a Howard Johnson's," Russell explained. "Long before your time. They had them all over the country. The best ice cream sodas, and these famous hot dogs on crooked toast buns."

In a way it excited him to be back at Howard Johnson's, even though it wasn't really Howard Johnson's anymore. Nothing being what it had been. Russell sat a moment getting his bearings. He felt a pang. Howard Johnson's – it symbolized his generation. Many a high school romance, or at least the hopes of one, got started over a Howard Johnson's ice cream soda.

"Howard Johnson's," Billy piped up.

"See, Billy remembers Howard Johnson's."

"I don't like it," said Tad. "Where does it say Howard Johnson? Who was he? Some president?"

"*Johnson's* not Johnson," said Billy.

The kid laughed in his goofy way. "It says Peony. Looks like a crap hole to me. Those colors stink together."

"Since when have you developed taste?" said Sonia.

"Orange and green. Makes my stomach hurt. Even that last place was better than this. Billy's flophouse. We should've stayed right there, it was nice in that town."

"The place with the cum stains?" said Sonia.

"Eat my farts," Billy chimed in.

"Well, Sonia, you should know," said Tad.

"What do you mean?"

"Ask Russell."

"Ask me what?"

"Where are we?" said Billy.

"Howard Johnson," said Tad. "We just been through all that."

"HO-JO'S? I love HO-JO'S!" said Billy as if just awakening. "I love how they make them strawberry ice cream sodas. They plop that scoop over the side of the glass without it slidin' off." He was laughing wildly. "They keep the ice cream from slidin' off! That's the trick pony!"

Russell drove up to the vertical OFFICE sign in orange neon.

"I hate to give you the bad news, Billy, but there's no ice cream at this place," Tad told him.

"Whaddaya mean?"

"Christ, Tad, he was finally happy again, now you have to go and spoil it." Sonia got out slamming the car door.

Russell flinched. Don't slam the door. Leo's door. He didn't need broken door hinges along with everything else.

"I want an ice cream soda. Strawberry," said Billy.

"Egg rolls is what you're gonna get here," said Tad.

"Egg rolls! I hate egg rolls! Depise 'em. They're made from rats and alley cats."

CHAPTER 60

Horrible

The kids pushed past Russell to get inside the Peony. "It's freezing here," Tad was saying. "So far this is the coldest state." Russell elbowed him away from the front desk.

"Hey! Maybe they give massages," said Tad. "That wouldn't be so bad. I'd like a massage from a Peony girl who'd walk on my back then give me a blow job. Wouldn't you Billy?"

The desk clerk with the dark greasy hair chuckled.

Peaches said, "You disgust me."

"He's gross," said Sonia. The girls took off for the room, Tad going after them yelling *wait*.

Russell finished the check-in, then took Billy by the arm. Slowly they moved down the hallway. "Do you think they have naked massage girls?"

"I don't know Billy."

"I need to touch some pussy."

Russell took a deep breath. "Yeah. We'll have to see what's what, OK?"

The old man looked up at him in a way that made Russell uneasy. I'm not a god, he thought, I cannot provide all things to all people.

CHAPTER 61

Needs

A big argument had broken out over the sleeping arrangements. Peaches, no longer willing to share a bed with Tad, was saying she'd share with Billy.

"Like hell you will," said Russell walking in on the conversation. He had the old man in tow. "Billy gets his own bed and his own room. The three... that is the rest of you..." He paused, sucking in his bottom lip. Now that he'd slept with Sonia it was difficult lumping her in with the others. He wished he could say: Sonia comes with me.

Billy, usually quick to jump in, remained silent.

"The only other option is for Peaches and Sonia to share," Russell said finally.

It was a terrible situation. Now Sonia wouldn't be able to slip out of bed and into his room without waking up Peaches. He wanted Peaches in bed with Tad so that Sonia was free to come and go if she wanted to. He was hoping she wanted to. He couldn't get a read on the situation. He wondered if Clara might be able to help, maybe tell him how Sonia is feeling. But Clara probably thinks he's reached Niagara Falls by now.

"You don't understand, Billy needs me," Peaches was saying. "I can look after him. What if something happens in the night, nobody will even know or be able to help him. It could be horrible for Billy."

"It could be horrible," the old man repeated.

"Billy-goat," Tad squawked. He'd kicked off his sneakers, flapping his head and rolling his eyes – his pathetic goat imitation. Then taking two wire hangers out of the closet he began twisting them together.

"Billy, I'm making you moose antlers," he said.

"Billy-goat," the old man repeated.

Lately he'd taken to repeating phrases, but usually those that would benefit him.

"I sleep in the room right next to his, with the door open practically every night," said Russell. "I'll keep an ear out for Billy."

Those times a connecting room wasn't available felt like his birthday. When Sonia had shown up unexpectedly, Russell immediately shut the door between rooms. By then BBW was out so cold it almost didn't matter.

"I think..."

He glared at Tad. "Forget it. Billy sleeps alone."

Leaning on the walker, the dirty camel hair coat hung off his bony frame. The old man started whimpering. "I need my Shelley Lee, I need my little girl."

Russell could see the hunger for Peaches in the old eyes. It made him even more unglued. Basically he didn't know these kids from a hole in the ground. Suppose Billy did something stupid and Peaches turned on him? It seemed unlikely but who could say? When it came to people you couldn't be sure of anything. Maggie taught him that. He'd loved, honored and obeyed. He still got screwed.

Sonia, just standing by quietly during all the fuss, was making him hot. Just standing there. Russell felt himself grow hard. He wished he could blurt out the same things Billy did. He wished he could say *I want to fuck Sonia*. But by the time you get to do that, what do you have left? Your balls are shot.

Dinner at The Rustic Shanty was a misery. Nobody happy about anything. They hated the rough wall paneling which Russell found interesting. Billy claiming the knots in the wood housed bugs. The chairs were uncomfortable, someone got a used dirty napkin, they all hated the food. "Pack everything for takeout, please," Russell told the waitress. She looked at him sympathetically. Maybe he should invite her along. She seemed the type who could whip these kids into shape. They even hated the music coming out of the jukebox. And of course the sleeping arrangements which they bickered about all during dinner. Billy making the one positive comment. "I like that cute paper fan."

"Fan? What fan?" said Tad scratching his head and looking around.

"You got dandruff," Billy told him.

CHAPTER 62

Blind

Back in the room Billy was cooing over the fan on his wall. "Ain't that just the cutest thing. Reminds me of the time we toured Korea with my band. I had every whore in that country bangin' down my door. Those gals sure know what they're doin'. The ones who give the massage are blind."

"So that's the big deal fan?" Sniffing inside his doggie-bag, Tad's head jerked up. "Blind massage? How can they know where to touch?"

"And, where not to touch," Sonia added, a smile playing across her lips.

Russell picked up on it. A signal? For later? He was desperate for her, wondering if the feeling was mutual.

"It's bliss," BBW was saying. "Everywhere you want they put their hands and little tongues. It's bliss. One little cute one with coal-black eyes put her thumb up my crack."

Howling, Tad fell across the bed.

"Settle down! You want them to throw us out?"

"Ko-rea," Billy went on. "It was heaven. Not like this trip. This lousy bum-fuck trip with no fuckin'."

Tad continued laughing. "There's some fucking going on, going on. But not by you or me, Billy."

The old man furrowed his brow. His white whiskers had grown thicker, Peaches trimming them into a short, pointed beard that made him look like a wizard. "I don't wanna fuck you," he told Tad.

"That isn't what I meant!"

"We know what you meant," said Russell putting his half of foil-wrapped cheeseburger on the dresser. "How'd you like to step outside?"

On his back on the bed with his hands folded behind his head Tad hooted. "You're going to fight me over Sonia? Sonia's reputation? You're bullshitting me, dude."

Russell stepped closer to the bed.

"Stop it!" Sonia shook him by the arm. "This isn't the wild west, I can handle my own reputation, thank you very much. Have you both gone crazy?"

"Men are generally crazy," said Peaches. She'd been sucking down a chocolate milkshake she brought back from dinner. The straw fell out and some slopped onto the bedspread. "Oh, darn."

"That's sloppy drinkin' Shelley Lee."

Then everyone looked at everyone.

"In Africa where my ancestors came from, that is originally," said Peaches, "the men did terrible things to the other men. And to the women and children. The tribes were always at each other. They still are. Why does it have to be this way? Why do men have to fight over everything? Why can't they talk things out?"

That's right, thought Russell, looking down on Tad who was smirking. We men have to fight things out. It's never going to change.

"I don't want to fight you, dude. I'll slaughter you. I'm young and you're not. Plus you got those arms..."

"These arms," and Russell pushed up his sleeve to make a muscle.

Billy whistled. "That's a good one."

"Wow, dude, I'm almost impressed. But I still don't want to fight you. I'll cream you, then who'd drive the car? Peaches? Sonia?"

Russell crossed his arms. "How about this. You beat me, you get to drive. How about it?" Russell hadn't realized just how badly he wanted to get his hands on the kid. He'd been sitting on it. Literally.

"Tad is DUI," said Peaches.

Russell let out a laugh. "That figures. What were you under the influence of?"

Tad turned his head on the pillow. Finally muttering, "I was under the influence."

The room had become quiet. Then Peaches squashed the empty milkshake container.

"I had this nervous breakdown. I gave up all the stuff, even beer. And I had this nervous breakdown. I told you I need my stuff! I can't make it without my little buzz. That night I slid. Had some tequila with the worm. A lot of tequila."

"You eat the worm?" said Billy.

The girls screeched.

"No, this other guy, Phil, he did. I drank till closing then crashed into a tree."

Jesus, thought Russell. "Did anyone get hurt?"

"I was by myself. I felt so good that night, hadn't felt that good in a long time." The kid paused. "The whole time they had me locked up. They fed me so many *dopey-pills* all I could do was sit around watching TV. The common room they call it. Man those couches were the worst! Fucking hard plastic. Cold in the winter and hot in the summer. You could never get comfortable in that place."

So the kid spent time in the bin. It had to be more than just giving up drugs. But Tad clammed up. He wasn't telling. For a second, maybe two, Russell had felt mildly interested.

"I was in the Gulf War, they were blowing things up. If you think you had it bad. At least you came out alive. A lot of soldiers didn't."

"I'm not comparing."

Russell sat down in a chair by the window. Beating up the kid felt lame now. "Let's finish eating," he said reaching for what was left of his burger.

"I want my blind massage," said Billy.

CHAPTER 63

Wings

The Peony Motor Inn did supply massage girls, and boys, if you wanted them. The kids were in agreement: Billy should have his massage. Russell felt too worn down to protest. "Do what you want, just keep me out of it."

He shut the door between his room and Billy's, took a hot shower and got into bed. The room was a strange, dark metallic blue that made him think of the underside of tropical bird wings. He'd been mildly disappointed – anticipating the orange and green HO-JO color scheme.

From the other side of the wall Russell could hear giggling. Wondered if Billy was being stroked and pummeled by the hands of some exotic creature – at least by Peony standards. The kids, he hoped, were standing by, making sure the old man didn't do anything out of line. Not sure what that even meant under the circumstances, Russell fell into a restless sleep.

❧

Nina was phoning again. Leaving messages threatening an *all points alarm*. "I'll track you down in every state," she spat into the phone. She was capable. Like Stan said: It's a quandary. More than ever, now. Now that he'd slept with Sonia, and wanted to again, how could he dump the kids? He'd have to keep ducking Nina.

When his alarm went off at seven he wanted to turn over and sleep for a solid month. Without bothering to shave or brush his teeth Russell threw on his clothes.

In Billy's room the kids had already ordered room service breakfast, trays and dishes littering the floor and across the dresser. BBW was reclined against the pillows and looking a lot better since his massage. A lot better than I do, thought Russell. "You look well," he told the old man.

"It really brought the life back to him!" Peaches was squealing with joy.

"Y'all should get one!" BBW was saying.

"I think we should stay here a while," said Tad. "I like it here at the Peony."

"Well the Peony doesn't like you," said Russell.

"According to you, there's no place that likes us." Tad punched a pillow. "No place! Anywhere. Ever."

Tough shit, thought Russell. "We're checking out in ten minutes so collect your gear and let's move it."

Now he felt in charge all the time. Even if it was just an old cranky man and three kids. During their marriage, Maggie had been in charge, mostly, then the army. Even Stan had power over him, often telling him what he should do. In some ways even his old mother. Not anymore.

"Bet you haven't had your breakfast yet," said Sonia.

He felt himself softening. She must be thinking of him. It was small, but it was big. "I'll grab something on the road."

Sonia's nipples showed through her pale-blue T, the low-rise jeans exposing more than a few inches of soft white back and belly; jeans riding almost too low. When she bent over to lace her sneaker, he saw the shadow of her crack.

They both knew he was looking.

Russell's head snapped up. "Don't go anywhere," he told them, heading for the door. "We're leaving in five minutes."

From the lobby he phoned Stan. No answer. It was past nine so he phoned the plant. When nobody answered the main switchboard Russell felt confused, letting it ring another few minutes. What happened at the plant? Evacuated? He pictured Stan and the other electrical workers huddled outside in cold rain (Stan said it had been raining non-stop). Russell pictured everyone outside with no coats or umbrellas. Stan and the men getting soaked while the buildings were combed by robots in HAZMAT suits, and sniffing German Shepherds.

Then he remembered. Saturday.

CHAPTER 64

Not That Smart

For exactly how long Russell sat in the room chair, he did not know. Not by hours, halves or minutes. He sat by the window though there was no view. A parking lot, a couple of smoke stacks in the distance. That was it. He felt exhausted. Strung out. He felt like Billy without the food stains.

Be at home, Stan, he was thinking, punching in the number again. Stan didn't always answer his cell which was annoying. Especially under the current circumstances.

When his brother finally picked up, Russell said, "Are you alone?"

"Sure! Why'd you ask? Hey what's going on? Where you calling from now?"

He stared at the paper fan splayed and mounted over the bed, the same fan that was in Billy's room, and the kids'. Probably in every room of this godforsaken motel. Across the folds was a message in Chinese characters. A message of hope? *You will have all the lotus blossoms life can offer* – that sort of thing? Or did they have a fire-sale here in Iowa on paper fans? Some salesman going door-to-door, motel to motel. Do people even go *door to door* anymore? When they first got married, Maggie sold Mary Kay Cosmetics. She was desperate to score enough points to win the big pink Cadillac.

"Bro, you still there?" said Stan breaking his spell.

"Listen, if you screwed Nina I need to know right away."

"Wait a minute."

"No, Stan, no minute. Now! Tell me if you and Nina fucked."

"She gave me a blow job, that's all. She didn't want me to fuck her, she was bleeding."

"How many times?"

"How many times what?"

"How many times were you with her?"

"Just the one. What is this, an interrogation? Since when do you care who I fuck?"

"So you did fuck her!"

"No! No! I used *fuck* generically, like vitamins. Meaning, you know, sex. What's going on with you, Russell? You sound half-nuts."

"I sound half-nuts? That's a good one. Maybe I am half-nuts. Maybe I belong in the nut house, too."

"You're saying I should go in the nut house for one measly blow job?"

Russell leaned back in the chair studying his fingers. The nails were too long. Stiff. They'd gotten thick; sort of yellowish. It might be a nail fungus. It could also be a distortion from the strange blue walls that felt slippery even in the daytime.

"Stan, you know I'm in trouble here, it's not like I haven't kept you informed. You had to go and fuck around with Nina? She's my employer. I've got Leo's car, and Leo can be dangerous."

"I still don't see where I fit in."

"I need someone I can trust. Totally. Now that you've slept with Nina... well it puts me off, Stan. It puts me off."

"It was just the once! A five minute BJ and off she toddled. She's an ugly one. You know I like the pretty ones and that one is... I didn't even watch. You know how I like to watch. I closed my eyes and made believe it was Clara doing me."

Clara again! "I thought you could have Clara whenever you wanted."

"Noooo. That stopped last summer. She got real finicky, always wanting me to take a shower first, wouldn't even let me grab her without using those antibacterial hand wipes. It got annoying. *Very* annoying."

"Stan do you swear you only had Nina that one time?"

"I swear. On Mom's life."

Russell wasn't sure that necessarily constituted a solemn vow (Mom annoyed Stan as much as she annoyed him). But he and Stan were a million miles apart. At least thousands of miles. He had no choice. He'd have to accept Stan's word as pledge.

"I trust you," said Russell.

"Of course you can trust me. You know, you hurt my feelings back when you were saying that stuff."

"I know, I know. I'm a mess. I fucked Sonia and I haven't been the same."

"Maybe that's a good thing."

A good thing. Russell hadn't considered it. How could he? How could he consider anything good, with Nina hot on his trail and Denver still a dot on the map?

"Nina keeps phoning, says she's putting the cops and the dogs on me. What should I do?" He rested his heels on the edge of the bed.

"OK. Let me think. OK, OK. Here's what you do. You phone Nina, and you tell her you've been traveling through some pretty remote territory. You know, remote. Places with no cell reception. No towers. And that you tried and tried to phone her, but you finally only got reception today. Today for the first time."

"She'll never believe me."

"Sure she will. I'm telling you, she's not that smart. She does the smarty-pants routine but it's only an act. They're both stupid, she and that brother."

"What!" He scrambled to his feet. "You met Leo?"

"Just for a second! When I dropped her off at the car place. You know, after the BJ. She had no wheels, she took a bus to your house."

"She runs a freakin' car service how can she have no wheels?"

"You know, I asked her that same thing and she said all her cars were out."

Russell pulled the window blind up to the top. "I don't think it's going to snow today," talking more to himself. "It's almost a miracle. I never want to see snow again. When this trip is over..." If it's ever over... He stood squinting at the sky.

"You still there?" he could hear Stan saying.

"When this trip is finally over I may move to Florida."

"You and Clara! That's what she keeps saying. Too many hurricanes down there. She keeps talking about Florida oranges. And those pastel cottages."

Russell didn't know from pastel cottages. But Florida oranges sounded clean and refreshing. "I need a big, big change," he said. "By the way, I slept with Sonia. Did I mention that?"

"This is news to me!" Stan laughed. "You already told me."

"I have feelings for her, Stan. It isn't good, she's like a kid. She is a kid. Technically she could be my kid." He pulled the string on the blind and it came crashing down.

"That's why you like it," Stan said.

"You saying I'm a perv?"

"Not exactly. She's yours to boss around and screw at the same time. Every man's dream. Sort of like that old joke about the mute woman with no teeth whose father owns a liquor store. The perfect woman."

"I could never relate to that joke," said Russell.

CHAPTER 65

Whatever She Wants

The old man was asleep in his coat per usual when Russell returned to the room. The kids, watching TV, barely glanced up.

Tad said, "Russell is there any way..."

"We're not staying."

Sonia was lying on her stomach, chin resting in her hands. "This is a very interesting show," she said, "about the waterfalls in Iowa. I had no idea they had any here, I didn't expect them I guess. I bet they're beautiful in person. I've never seen a live waterfall."

"Or a dead one," said Tad.

"I'd like to see one," said Sonia rolling onto her side. She fixed him with a look. "Russell, do you think we could stop by one?"

He stood in the doorway rubbing his chin stubble, watching Billy's chest rise and fall under the coat. He sighed. "If it's on the way I guess we could. We'd have to find one that's on our route, I can't deviate much, it will add to the time."

"Sonia's on top of you," said Tad.

Russell's eyes narrowed. Again with the digs?

"I already got a brochure from the desk," Sonia was saying, "listing all the waterfalls in Iowa." She held up a glossy printed folder. "See. They look très magnifique."

Très magnifique? The Frenchie thing! What is it with these women and the Frenchie thing? thought Russell.

He swallowed down hard. "OK. I'll take a look. When we stop for lunch, I'll see what's what. How's that?"

Tad made smooching noises. "Sonia gets whatever she wants."

She kicked him in the leg and he yelped. "That hurt!"

"I get what I want because I deserve it," said Sonia.

"I never get what I want," said Peaches. "Most black people never get what they want, their whole lives. It's so sad. Why do you suppose that is?"

"I don't know," said Russell. He was thinking about all the loot she wrangled out of Billy.

"I want another massage!" yelled Billy, suddenly wide awake.

❧

For a change it wasn't snowing and Russell was able to drive at a decent rate of speed. The kids were passing around waterfall brochures. Before they left the Peony, Peaches snatched a handful more from the lobby rack. "So many waterfalls in Iowa," she said. "There's got to be one we can see, wouldn't you think, Russell?"

"It sounds like it might possibly work." He wasn't promising anything.

"Most are in the state parks," Tad was saying. "It's corrupt."

Sonia groaned. "How can a waterfall be corrupt? That's the most ridiculous thing I've ever heard. You'll do anything to be the opposite of me, won't you, Tad? I say black you say white. I say day you say night."

"Sonia's a poet and she don't know it."

"Tad, you can be very childish," said Peaches. "You're jealous because Sonia came up with the waterfall idea first."

"It was my idea," said Billy.

Everyone laughed. "At least he didn't give credit to Shelley Lee," said Tad.

At lunch in a café called The Gingham, where the curtains and menus and paper place mats were done up red and white checkered, they passed brochures around the table, each selling the strengths of their desired waterfall.

Billy wanted to see one called *Beulah Spring Falls* because he once had a maid named Beulah.

Peaches said it was totally racist to call anyone, or anything, including a waterfall, *Beulah*. "In this day and age, can you imagine," she said. "It's a slave name."

She was pushing *Bridal Veil Falls* which she claimed looked much nicer on the brochure, and had a lovely name reminding you of a beautiful bride.

"The Bride of Frankenstein," said Tad. *Woodman Hollow Falls* got his vote, it reminded him of the headless horseman of Sleepy Hollow. Tad was convinced they'd see his ghost there.

Russell ordered a grilled hot dog and coffee. He was beginning to understand more of why Tad ended up in the psycho ward. Sonia ordered black coffee and nothing more, saying she felt tired and not remotely hungry, speaking up in favor of *Malanaphy Spring Falls* because it reminded her of a Native American name. Plus she was kind of hoping they might sell a turquoise hair clip from a little souvenir booth. She said, "I've always wanted a real turquoise hair clip. To match the necklace Billy bought me."

"I'll get you one, Sonia darlin'," said Billy.

"That's exactly what I mean, it's all corrupt." Tad was separating the ham from the cheese in his sandwich. "Cheese is very unhealthy." He wrapped it in a napkin. "The minute they sell things at a natural wonder it becomes corrupted."

Sonia began laughing in a way that didn't sound particularly friendly. "Is corrupt a new word for you? Did you sit up all night studying the dictionary?"

Biting into the hot dog, Russell pictured his giant WEBSTER on the oak stand in his dining room. Unused for so long, the pages were probably dry and yellowing.

"I slept like a lamb, Sonia darlin'. What did you do?" said Tad.

"I slept like a lion." Baring her straight white teeth she growled. "Which waterfall do you like Russell?"

Spreading more mustard on the hot dog, it hit him like a punch. His knife clattered to the floor. Niagara!

"Jeez, Russell, pretty sloppy," said Tad.

Niagara! That's a waterfall! He had told Stan that Clara was way off base. She pictured him at a waterfall, just the wrong one. What else did Clara say? He doubted Stan would remember. Now he definitely had to phone her. It was too coincidental to be a coincidence. Russell felt a new found respect for her powers where he used to think she was flaky. Maybe there's more to Clara than meets the eye, he thought. Maybe she is a true visionary.

What else had he been wrong about? A sobering thought. Nina? Had he been wrong about her? Immediately telling himself: Not Nina! Even Stan said Nina was dumb; also mean if you read between the lines.

He wished he could give Stan a brotherly bear hug. Share some booze and cigars. A few laughs. He felt lonely in a way he could only describe as dehydration – the liquids in his body siphoned off into the tank of Leo's car: fueling it, them, all five of them, into some slot known only as *later*. He almost started crying. He stared into his coffee until the feeling subsided.

Sonia placed a hand on his arm. "Do you have a favorite waterfall?"

He raised his head slowly. The gingham curtains gyrating before his eyes made a crazy zig-zag that he knew couldn't be for real. Tapping his arm, Sonia was encouraging him to pick *her* favorite waterfall. He knew that, too.

CHAPTER 66

Denied

I am so fucking blown thought Russell climbing behind the wheel. Dancing curtains. Very bad sign. It finally caught up with him. Plus, in the last twenty-four hours, the car had made this permanent switch in his mind to *Leo's car*. As if Leo were huddled under the hood controlling the pistons and gears. Seized by fear that he knew was irrational, he was doing his best to appear normal. While Billy and the kids became more and more psyched over seeing a waterfall.

"It's just spring water tumbling over rock," Russell said.

He drove onto another grinding highway. Lots of truck traffic. The sky overcast. The kids wouldn't shut up about the waterfall. They weren't about to be denied.

"If we don't do something different soon I'll blow my brains out," said Tad.

Both of us, thought Russell. The kid unfortunately sitting up front again.

"I need to experience new things," Peaches was saying.

Russell smelled something overly sweet permeating the car. Whatever it was, it was starting to give him a headache. "Is that perfume I smell?"

"It's important," Peaches went on. "Otherwise life becomes routine, and stale. Same old same old. That's why I switched perfumes. And boyfriends. That's why I'm with Billy now."

"You're with me," said Billy. "I'm old."

A roar went up – *no way, Billy, no way are you old*! When the kids finally quieted, Sonia added: "No matter what we say there's no getting around it. Billy is definitely old."

"That's right, Sonia darlin'. Only a true vampire could say it so suck-sinkly."

"Sonia, you are a vampire, a mean mean vampire, that's what there's no getting around," said Tad.

"Watch out she'll suck your blood!" Billy cackling out his notion of vampire noises.

"Why do you call her darlin' every other word, Billy? And buy her anything she wants?" Tad's voice sounding muffled.

"Quit picking your nose in the car," said Russell.

"Sonia's a darlin'," the old man said.

"I guess if you like vampires."

"I like 'em."

"That beard," Tad was saying. "I don't know, it's making you look, I don't know, kind of something."

"Junkyard dog. I look like a junkyard dog." BBW became ecstatic. "I used to love that song!"

"Ah," said Tad blowing him off with a wave. "So that's it. So which waterfall is it going to be? Huh? Woodman Hollow?"

"No, no, Bridal Veil!" Peaches shouted from the back seat.

"That one sucks!" said Tad.

"Calm down all of you. I haven't found one on the route yet."

"The route, always the route." Tad was bending toward the floor.

Russell smelled burning sulfur. "Who lit a match?"

"Guess," said Peaches.

"Try it again and you're out of the car, Tad. If I said it once, I said it a hundred times. There's no smoking in this car." In Leo's car. Russell felt a shiver move through him.

"Then take us to a waterfall! Take us today, Russell, we want to go today! Not tomorrow or next week. We want it now, while we all feel the same. Not when somebody here changes their mind and wants to go shopping."

"Russell would you like a stick of gum?" Sonia holding it over his shoulder.

"Go on, bribe him Sonia. More corruption. I don't understand..."

"It's not for you to understand." Russell feeling her fingertips when he took the stick of gum.

"Y'all make me puke," said Billy. "I'm sick of every one a you. You're all spoilt. That's yer problem."

Great, thought Russell, he's sick of the kids. Now he'll want to chuck them out, just when things are possibly getting back on track with Sonia. He popped the gum in his mouth. Maybe it was all part of her plan to freshen his breath. For later. Chomping loudly, so Sonia could hear her gum in his mouth, he was planning a direct hit. A bottle of chilled white wine. He'll pick it up from a liquor store during lunch. Pass her a note to come to his room for some wine. That should loosen things up. Though Sonia didn't need any loosening that other time. Loose as a goose, he slipped right in.

CHAPTER 67

Anti-what

At dinner they nagged him to death until he finally agreed. Tomorrow they would see a waterfall.

"Only one. And we're not spending the whole day." Studying the menu he watched Sonia from the corner of his eye. He saw her smile like a cat; a wise one; the kind who knew which walls held mice.

"Thanks, Russell," she said. "From all of us."

Show me with your body, he thought.

He put the menu on his lap. He'd started leaking.

She didn't come to him that night, though after dinner he slipped the note into the pocket of her ski jacket; Sonia smiling briefly, looking down at her pocket. She knew without reading it. She didn't show up. Maybe Peaches had awakened when Sonia slid out of the bed they shared. Or maybe she never intended to come. Maybe she used him that one time for her own pleasure, and that was that.

Sometime before dawn he jerked off in bed, her face and body tight in his mind. And to hell with the cum stains on the sheets.

At breakfast he couldn't look at her. She acted normal enough eating her way through a stack of blueberry pancakes. Tad said, "Sonia's got her appetite back. She's eating like a lumberjack." The kid smirking.

"Just getting my energy up for the falls. Blueberries are loaded with antioxidants."

"Anti-what?" Billy's eyes bugged out of his head. "Sonia darlin', that's not antifreeze you're pourin' over those flapjacks?" The old man started to tremble so badly he knocked over the sugar packet bowl.

Russell stood up. "Tad put them back," he said.

The old man was in a state. He cried out, "Shelley Lee not the antifreeze! I'm beggin' you." Tears streaming down his face.

Familiar enough with Billy's outbursts, the kids continued eating as Russell made his way around the table. He squatted next to the old man. "What's the matter?"

Billy was in a state. "Shelley Lee not the antifreeze!" he screamed out again.

Was Billy hallucinating, or did Shelley Lee actually *off herself* by drinking antifreeze? It was too hideous to consider. Russell saw guys do things during the war, to get sent home. Chopped off toes, superficial gunshot wounds... but nobody drank antifreeze. Not that he heard about.

"Billy, Billy, take it easy," he said. "Tad will you straighten out that damn sugar bowl."

People in the breakfast room were looking in their direction. "Billy, that's maple syrup Sonia's pouring on her pancakes. See the little blueberries in the pancakes? Blueberries are healthy for you." He was afraid to mention *antioxidants*, that Billy would flare up again.

The old man pointed at the pancakes. "It ain't the blueberries worryin' me."

"We understand," said Peaches stroking his hand.

He yanked it away. "Don't take liberties girl!"

"I would never."

"Shut up, Shelley Lee! I won't hear anymore of your gibberish. You want to be a man, go on, be a man. Cut off your breasts and grow a dick. Let's see what kinda man you are."

Peaches squealed sharply, looking toward Russell. He shook his head and put up a warning finger. For once they all seemed to understand. Nobody uttered a syllable. Surprising. Even in the army, when the situation called for absolute silence, somebody would fart. The kids were stone statues around the breakfast table.

"What the hell's goin' on? What's the matter with everybody?" Billy looked around the table.

Tad grinned. "Not a durn thing, Billy-goat, everything is hunky dory. And it's not snowing!"

"Hunky dory. That's what I like! Let's get to the waterfall before it dries up. Or I dry up. Whichever comes first!"

CHAPTER 68

On The Route

Crane Pelon Falls happened to be on the route. Russell found it marked on the map but nobody wanted to go because there wasn't a brochure.

"That's how you plan your life, according to a brochure? If that's the case you're in trouble. We're going to Crane Pelon Falls. Get ready to leave here."

Nobody seemed remotely interested since it wasn't any falls they had considered. This is unreal, thought Russell. All that carrying on, and now they could care less.

Even Billy was quiet in the car; though he did ask for the radio turned up when Brenda Lee came on singing a Christmas song.

"She's dead, right?" said Tad.

"How'd you like to get your mouth washed out with soap?" Billy said.

Tad burped. "What did I do?"

"Everyone calm down, we're going to the falls," said Russell. "It won't be long. I'm sure they're as good as any other falls. Even better."

"Not as good as Beulah," said Billy. "Those are the best falls this side of the Mississippi. You ask anyone. Mark Twain. You ask him, he knew. He wrote about the Beulah Falls in one of them books, I think it was Huck Finn."

"Huck Finn! No way! No way did Huck Finn get anywhere near your Beulah Falls, Billy." Tad pounded the seat laughing.

"Whadda *you* know?" Billy shot back.

"Don't hit the seat," said Russell. That's all he needed, a tear in Leo's upholstery.

Almost missing the exit sign, making a hairpin turn at the last second, he followed the orange markers nailed to the trees, directing them toward Crane Pelon Falls. Another day without snow. Amazing. Was God actually listening for a change? Russell had prayed; but mostly to have Sonia again in bed with him. He wondered if that would be considered blasphemy?

The road climbed steep but deceptive. Cleared of snow, the blacktop surface glistened. Russell kept climbing (at least Leo's car did) which in itself was a kind of second miracle. Lately he sensed it losing power. As if its parts had ground down, worn themselves out, were about to throw in the towel and end up in the car graveyard. Leo's car (as Russell had come to know it) felt young in body (Leo had babied it) but old in spirit. During the past few weeks the car seemed to age, in that it even smelled old, like overripe cheese. Of course that could be coming from the piles of dirty clothes in plastic bags.

"The next town we hit a laundromat," he said.

"Russell I think you took a wrong turn." Tad was taking his sneakers off. "How could it take this long to reach the falls? Maybe those orange things are for something else. I don't see any waterfall. This is turning into another big waste of time."

"You have a pressing engagement?" Russell couldn't keep the sarcasm out of his voice. The girls laughed; then Billy, who seemed to have flipped back into his happy mode. At least for now. By the time this trip is over, we're all going to end up insane, thought Russell making another sharp turn.

CHAPTER 69

Wild and Crashing

Out of nowhere, as if they stepped across some mark, or drove straight into the Bermuda Triangle – the falls. Wild and crashing, majestic, just a few hundred yards ahead. He slowed Leo's car, lowering his window to take in the sight and sound of it. The rushing water – so powerful it could probably crush a man and he'd never feel it. Russell thinking *I've become a violent man.*

The girls were going out of their minds and Billy kept saying, "Will ya take a look at that! Will ya!"

He stopped the car, the kids jumping out and rushing toward the wooden guard rail. Left behind, Billy was shouting, "What about me? You forgot me! Come back, come back!"

"I'll get you out," Russell told him.

The old man was furious. "The nerve a them kids, I'm givin' them up!"

Russell took hold of his arm. "Here, hang on to me."

Outside the car he was still yelling. "Ya bunch a losers! Desert an old man for a waterfall! I hope ya drop dead, all of ya." His eyes were wet and streaming. In the pale winter sunlight, his face looked more lined and sagging.

"Billy, they meant no harm, they're just excited to see the falls. Stay here by the car and I'll get your walker, and you can get closer, too."

"I don't want to get closer!"

Ignoring this, Russell took the walker out of the trunk. Setting it on the ground he noticed the colored tape had started to dry out, unravelling into limp streamers. Pulling it toward the old man he said, "Here you go."

Billy refused to look at him, or the walker, or even take hold of the thing.

"You can't see the falls without your walker," Russell said. "This is rough ground, there's a lot of rock. Even with your walker it's going to be tricky. You have to go carefully, OK? I'll hold your elbow."

"Don't touch me, Sonny!"

"Ah jeez." He looked into Billy's face. It seemed wiped clean, blotted out of its colorful history. "You may never get here again," said Russell; thinking *that's for sure*. "It would be a shame to miss the falls up close."

"I seen more waterfalls than you got fingers and toes."

The old man and his old clichéd lines. He was so tired of hearing them. "Hey!" he yelled to the kids. "Get over here and help Billy! Right now! Over here! Now!"

When nobody made a move, or even turned around, he wondered if all the noise from the falls had blotted him out, as well?

"I guess we'll have to do this on our own Billy." Taking the old man by the arm Russell pulled him toward the walker, placing his stiff fingers, one by one, around the metal bar. More or less dragging him along the path. All the while Billy claiming he could care less.

Then Peaches turned around, her dark eyes shining, her face wet from the falls churning moisture into the air. "Isn't it awesome!" Sonia, he noticed, had the same wet sheen, but on her light skin it was less obvious. His desire to lick her face was strong.

"Billy do you like the falls?" Peaches slipping her arm through his.

"Get off me, I know your kind."

Russell shook his head. "It might be best to leave him alone for now."

"I didn't mean anything." Hurt and confused she took her arm back as if she didn't know where to put it; finally putting her hands in her pockets. Boy can I relate to that, thought Russell. He often felt uneasy about where to put his arms, especially around strangers. Most of the time he shoved them in his pockets. That particular position, crook of the arm, created an optical illusion. In those moments his arms were of normal length. Though sooner or later they had to come out, be what they were.

"This is really something." Tad couldn't stop yawning. "Completely boring, just a lot of water."

"Are you out of your mind? It's a spectacle of nature!" Sonia was radiant. "I wish I had a camera. Look up there how the frozen water clings to the rocks. The rocks are the most amazing colors. Some even purple."

"So big deal, a purple rock." Tad turned away moving toward the car. "Use your cell camera."

"He has problems," Peaches announced.

"He's plain mean. Every time you feel sorry for him you become his co-dependent," said Sonia. "Naturally I can use my cell, I know that. But film would be a whole lot better."

"Stop arguing. You wanted to see the falls and now you stand around arguing," said Russell. "It's a disgrace."

He wasn't sure why he said that. Or if it was even true. Why should arguing at the falls be a disgrace? He remembered some Major dressing down some Corporal, saying something or other was a disgrace. He couldn't remember specifically. Anyway, why should something from ancient history even matter? He felt his phone vibrating in his shirt pocket and without looking knew: Nina. Her presence inside his phone, his pocket. She was a growth forming cells under his skin.

"These falls are truly amazin'," Billy was saying.

He seemed recovered. Though Russell didn't care for the look in his eyes. He looked shocked; like he put his knife in a toaster and somehow survived.

"I never dreamed they'd be so durn pretty, these falls," Billy went on. "They are just the prettiest thing."

"I love it here," said Sonia. "I wish we could camp out and fall asleep to the sound of the falls. It's like exciting music. I've never experienced anything quite like it."

"I could go to sleep here." Holding on to his walker, Billy's head dropped forward.

"Wake up!" Russell shook him by the arm. "You don't get to fall asleep out here, no way."

"I need to pee."

Wouldn't you know it. Russell scanned the area but tourist facilities looked shut down tight. Of course, it's winter. Or, winner. "I don't think there's a Mens Room open."

"I got to pee."

"What about your bag?" Russell didn't understand the old man's constant urge to pee. Didn't it automatically flow into his bag? Once or twice he'd thought about questioning Billy, to get it straight. But then he really didn't want the details.

"Full. It's full. And startin' to hurt. Bad."

Russell felt confused. How could a bag hurt?

"I'll help you," Sonia was saying.

"Sonia darlin'."

"How can you help him?" asked Russell.

"My dad had a suprapubic catheter. It used to clog all the time. I know what to do, I know how to get it unstuck. It can be very painful if it's left clogged."

"Very painful," Billy repeated. Thankfully Tad wasn't nearby to call him Billy-goat.

"You mean what Billy calls his super pubic tube?"

"Same thing."

"I can't stand it if you're in pain." Peaches' eyes welling up.

"Go wait in the car," Russell told her. When she seemed reluctant to leave, he waved her away. "Go! Go!"

"Good," said Sonia. "We don't need her. Do we Billy?"

The old man shook his head looking up at Sonia adoringly.

"Russell, you wait in the car too. This won't take very long."

He rubbed his stubble. He'd stopped shaving, thinking there wasn't much point. Who'd notice? In fact, all their grooming had slipped a notch; Billy's by about twenty notches.

"Isn't it too cold, to be, you know?" He looked around the area. "Fiddling with his stuff?"

Looking serious Sonia said, "What choice do we have? We can't leave him in pain."

"I'm in pain."

"Are you sure, Billy?" Russell hoping the whole thing was another scheme to gain attention. "You don't look in pain. I know you're full, I mean your bag, but you don't look in pain."

"Pain," said BBW.

Sonia nodded. Her eyes looking clear and determined. "He's in pain."

The day colder than Russell first realized.

"Wait in the car," she said.

Sonia was different, in charge now. Miniscule black flecks made her pale-blue irises appear cracked. Damaged. Then glued back together the way you fix a delicate porcelain vase. Still beautiful, yet the damage would always show. He had this sudden realization. That's Sonia.

"Russell, will you please go back to the car," she said again.

He took another look at the falls, the rushing wild freedom of it all. Then feeling anxious he moved in the direction of Leo's car.

CHAPTER 70

Nurse

In the back seat Peaches and Tad were snuggling. As if they'd never been on this trip, but were the same two people they used to be back in Ohio.

"I'll never figure any of you out if I live to be a hundred," Russell said.

"Don't worry, dude, Sonia used to be a nurse."

"What! Why the hell didn't she tell me?"

"She doesn't like to brag," said Peaches. "Her husband is a doctor, a famous heart surgeon."

Sonia has a husband. He sat at the wheel absorbing this. "She's married."

"Yes and no." Tad was laughing. Always laughing. Russell wanted to wring his throat.

"They're married but they don't live together. He's too busy and Sonia couldn't take the life. They met in the emergency room. But then Sonia wanted out, she hated the emergency room. *Too much bleeding for no good reason* was her excuse. And Edward's whole life is medicine. So they sorta split." Peaches looked solemn after her speech.

Edward. The man has a name. Russell raised a hand shielding his eyes though the sun had gone in again. An in again, out again day. He pictured Edward looming tall in his white doctor coat; white as the snow. Blinding. And, nurse Sonia. Also tall. It was starting to make a little sense. The casual way she acted about nudity, the casual sex. He'd felt something sterile, almost clinical around her. Not that Sonia couldn't stink up the car like the rest of them. But Russell had smelled her up close and personal. Clean, she smelled a little like Pine-Sol.

"You see there's nothing to worry about. Sonia will know what to do." Peaches making it all sound reassuring. "In med school she had to saw bodies apart to do those autopsies."

Tad interrupted. “It wasn’t a chain saw.”

“I didn’t say chain saw. But Sonia didn’t mind, she said it was interesting. But then she didn’t finish, instead she became a nurse.”

Med school? Autopsies? Sonia claimed to be twenty-three. Russell did the math. It didn’t add up. No wonder Billy called her a vampire. They all were. BBW had the instinct, even if he didn’t have the facts.

“What about you?” said Russell playing along. “Are you two secret rocket scientists?”

“We’re nothing and nobody,” said Tad. “Sonia is the big brain. But she’s afraid to be on her own... soooo... she moved in with us. Out of the slick condo, a very cool loft space. I don’t think Edward fucked her much. And she *has* known us practically her whole life.”

I guess that explains a few things, thought Russell; deciding it explained nothing. He snuck a peek at himself in the sun visor mirror. He didn’t look old or ugly. As for Sonia being married – who knows? Nothing these kids had to say could be taken at face value. He slammed the visor up. He never expected to be with her again. The one night she came to him she must’ve had an old urge for Edward, or someone. Some old urge. Closing her eyes and making believe. *Close your eyes and drink your wine.* Maggie said that once – soon after he came home from The Gulf. What was she doing while he was away defending his country?

He stared out at the diverging path. No sign of Sonia and Billy. She’d moved him somewhere, maybe behind a grove of trees for privacy. Not that anyone else was around taking a look at the falls. Just them. The five of them, seeing the falls in winter. It was a natural wonder. No matter what else went down, Russell would never forget.

“We’re going to leave as soon as Billy gets his tube done,” Russell told them. “I mean clear, gets his tube clear.” It seemed important to say it right. “So if you want to see the falls up close one more time this is your magic moment.”

Neither Peaches nor Tad said a single word or made a move to get out of the car. So much for their deep desire to see a waterfall. Russell tuned the radio to a sports channel. Another ten minutes went by. Suppose there was some problem with Billy’s apparatus, not as cut and dried as Sonia assured him. “This is taking longer than I expected,” he said.

“Dude, you worry too much. Sonia stopped a guy from dying

after he got shot by a gang member, right outside our apartment. You should have been there that night! Blasts! I thought bullets were gonna shatter the windows. She ran outside and knew how to stop the bleeding, kept him going till the EMS got there. Before Sonia came out he'd bled all over the street. I never knew a body could hold so much blood."

"He was a junkie from the neighborhood," said Peaches. "He could've had AIDS Sonia said. She wasn't even worried. She ran out and helped him. Sonia can be kind of like a saint. I guess from being *born again*."

The junkie may have had AIDS! Russell felt his body seize up. He didn't use a condom and she didn't suggest one. Why didn't Sonia warn him? Saint Sonia.

"Man she's practically suicidal, some of the crazy things she does." Tad was chewing. Russell smelled food, not fresh food. God knows how long that doggie-bag was stuffed back there.

With his mouth full Tad said, "This *is* taking a long time. She was faster with the gunshot wound."

"They could have gone for a walk after she fixed his tube. You know how sloooow Billy walks." One of them crinkled a plastic bag. "Maybe he wanted to see more of the falls, so they took a different trail."

Tad yawned. "Billy and his amazing technicolor walker. I hope they hurry 'cause I'm still starving. Give me one of those cookies," he said.

"There aren't any more, I ate the last one."

"I'm starving. This place has nowhere to eat. Nothing."

They continued to argue over the last cookie. Russell couldn't shake the junkie from his mind. He was starting to cramp in his legs. Was his blood count compromised? He growled saying to Tad, "I thought it was corrupt to have anything for sale at the falls? I guess that didn't include feeding your face." He turned in the seat to glare at him. Them. He felt taken. By all of them; even Billy. Most especially by Sonia. How could she? Unprotected sex after helping a bleeding junkie? He couldn't bend his mind around it.

"Yeah, well, I am pretty hungry," said Tad.

Russell slammed out of the car.

CHAPTER 71

Free At Last

You chop off a toe or a finger – you extricate yourself from hell. A soldier more or less put it that way. *Free at last*, said the soldier grinning and screaming from pain at the same time.

Russell ran toward the falls shouting Billy's name. He felt frantic, had no idea why he was running, just that he was, and tripping over sticks and branches and rocks on the trail. He kept shouting to Billy. Panting, he stopped to lean against the rail. Below, the churning water, looking whiter than snow, seemed almost magnified.

This was far more than spring water tumbling over rock – this was some miracle of nature. Or some watery hell they'd come to. The old man, for all practical purposes, gone. Into the woods like a disappearing wisp of smoke. Or a squirrel, he thought, staring overhead a moment, feeling vague, stirred by a dream you can't remember.

Over the roar of water, the trees seemed strangely still, their branches static, as if no squirrel or bird had ever lit down on them.

He noticed the big clouds were turning puffy. It could mean snow. Russell choked on his own phlegm. Where the hell was Billy? And Sonia? What had become of them?

CHAPTER 72

Swan Song

He returned again to the car. Opening the back door and sticking his head in. "I can't find them."

"That's funny," said Peaches. "Where could they be?"

"Ah jeez."

Russell felt the hairs stand up on his neck. "What does that mean, Tad?"

"Nothing much. Except... Well this one time Sonia talked about offing herself."

He yanked the kid out of the car. "You, too!" he told Peaches. She was slow to move. Russell screamed. She'd taken off her jacket, and when she finally stepped out, minus the jacket she was shivering, looking dazed. He leaned inside grabbing it, thrusting it at her. "We've got to find them!" He took off down the path pulling Tad along by the arm.

Complaining about the rough treatment, Tad was saying that Russell, as usual, was worried about nothing.

"Shut your mouth or I'll kill you. I'll kill you here and now. Understood?"

Tad froze.

"Move it!" Russell jerked him forward. The lump in his throat felt like a boulder blocking his airway.

"They shouldn't be too hard to find," said Peaches running close behind.

Let's hope so, he thought. Let's hope Sonia doesn't decide that today is her *swan song*. And, Billy's.

The trail climbed slightly then swung to the left, a split fork, one slice running parallel with the falls, the other, considerably more narrow, branching off into the woods. Russell stopped there. Put his hands on his knees leaning forward to catch his breath. He couldn't imagine Billy getting this far. How could he push the walker uphill? Even with Sonia's help. He felt a deep cold, the coldest of his life, move into his limbs. If Billy didn't make the climb what did it mean? He made the plunge? Billy would never kill himself. Yet for all practical purposes Billy was MIA.

Get a grip, Russell told himself. People went missing in action and died in wars. Not at the falls. Certainly not a blond they claimed was a nurse, and an old cranky man. Despite what Tad told him about Sonia's suicidal tendencies. "Goddammit!" They had to be around *somewhere*.

"Why are we standing here?" said Tad.

"I'm thinking."

"Oh you want to decide which trail. Why not flip a coin?"

"That's a great idea." Flip a coin over Billy's life. Sonia's, too. "How'd you like me to flip a coin over your life?"

"Mine ain't worth a buck."

"Every life has value." Peaches looked wistful. "You should never feel that life is worthless. It's a great gift. Look how the black people suffered and you don't hear me saying life is worthless. Do you?"

Tad, down on one knee lacing his boot, didn't seem to hear what she was saying; or chose not to.

"Life *is* a great gift," Russell heard himself saying. He smiled to reassure this nervous looking girl who looked younger every day; while the rest of them seemed to have aged on this goddamn road trip to hell. Even Sonia had been looking strained, thinner lately. Maybe she did plan on killing herself; had already done it. Taking Billy along for the ride.

What they'd all been doing for weeks. Just taking a ride.

Colorado lost in the shuffle of plastic bags, lousy food, bad motel rooms. Colorado – almost beside the point.

Russell buttoned his navy blue overcoat up to the neck. He turned up the collar.

"Next time, dude, bring a ski jacket."

Next time. What a joke. He stood there staring down both trails.

"I don't know what to do," said Russell. He felt his phone vibrating inside his coat pocket. He knew without knowing. Nina had the radar.

"Would you like me to take over?" Tad looked spacey, had probably ingested something in the car.

"No, I do not want you to take over." He coughed into his hand shaking off mucous.

"Gross, Russell! You're gonna spread germs in the car."

Ignoring this, he thought about phoning Stan. Or better yet, Clara. Clara might know where to find Billy and Sonia. He pointed at the kids. "You two go back and wait in the car."

"First you drag us out here now you don't want us."

"Just do what I say, dammit! Wait there. If Billy and Sonia show up, blast the horn so I'll know." He stared at the falls listening to the roar. "Blast it a bunch of times so I'll be sure and hear. You got that?"

"OK," said Peaches taking Tad by the hand.

Glued herself back onto Tad. Some girls are built that way. Can't go on without a man in their pocket. The body's not even cold, Russell wanted to say.

As soon as they made the turn and were out of sight, he grabbed his phone. The wind had picked up beating his hair around his face. How many weeks since he'd gotten a haircut? A steamy hot towel?

CHAPTER 73

Faith

Stan sounded cold and far away. As far as a person could be and still be reached; reachable. Russell deciding that made no sense.

"Billy's missing! Billy and Sonia! I need to speak to Clara, it's an emergency! You gotta give me her number, Stan."

"What do you mean they're missing?"

"We went to the falls, I mean we're at the falls, and Billy gets a clog in his tube and Sonia takes him away to fix it. Then they don't come back." He felt a pain shoot through his gut.

"What's she doing fixing Billy's tube? It doesn't sound Kosher."

"It's Kosher! Sonia's a nurse. I think she is." He scanned the distant trees. "Anyway she knows about that stuff, and they went off and now I can't find them. And Tad thinks Sonia might have killed herself."

"This is nuts! Why would a foxy chick like Sonia do that?"

"She may have AIDS. It's complicated. I need to find them and fast. Clara might know. She did know about the falls. She kept warning me about the falls and I didn't understand." Russell fumbled in his pocket for a tissue. Not finding any he coughed phlegm into the snow, noticing blood. Maggie's miscarriage crossed his mind. Their miscarriage. Quickly, he pushed all that away.

"Now I know, Stan. I know everything."

"Not quite."

"What do you mean?"

"Well you don't know where they are."

"Obviously! Obviously!"

"OK, get yourself in check." Stan sounded colder, even farther away, though his voice was coming through clear enough. "I'll give you Clara's number but she might not be home. That woman gets around."

"Stan for godsakes give me her cell."

"She might be doing a reading, if she's doing a reading she won't pick up."

"I'll take my chances!"

Stan rattled off her number, Russell repeating it back to avoid any margin for error. Already there'd been way too many margins for error.

"There's that other matter..." Stan was saying but Russell clicked off.

She picked up on the second ring, and he almost started bawling. "Clara, thank god. It's Russell and I'm in serious trouble."

"I've been waiting for you."

"Really?"

"You got to the falls."

"I'm here now. How did you know, Clara? Oh, never mind that, I can't find Billy. Or Sonia. Can you see them? In your psychic sense, can you see them anywhere?"

"I knew *that woman* would be the source," she said. "Sonia. Is that her name?"

"The source of what? Clara, can you visualize them? If Billy's dead, I may as well jump into the falls myself."

"Calm down." She sounded matter of fact. "Billy's not dead. Neither is Sonia. Not that that would be a big loss. But Billy would, I always liked his music. Very sweet, from the heart."

He gripped the guard rail with his free hand and felt some sense of relief. According to Clara at least Billy was not dead. Could he trust her? Could he trust anyone? "Then where is he?"

"I'm not sure. But he gave up something. Not his life," she added with a giggle. "Maybe his guitar?"

"He's not traveling with a guitar. Stan told you about Billy and his music?"

"Russell, you think I'm dense or something? You think I live in a cave? I just said I like his music. Are you sleep-walking?"

"Sorry. I'm very strung out right now. I'm very upset. I've got this responsibility, and now I can't find him. Or Sonia," he added lowering his voice.

"Do you want to find Sonia?"

"Of course, of course I do!"

"Hmmm."

"What's that s'posed to mean?" Exhausted, he leaned against the rail. The wind blew snow off the trees stinging his face.

"I'm getting that you don't really want to find Sonia. That you did, and now you don't. But you can't admit it. You like thinking of yourself as the big savior. It's a delusion, Russell."

"I have to find them both."

"If you give up Sonia, I may be able to help. She's blocking my energy."

"There's energy, you're getting energy?"

"I said it's blocked. Is she a blond?"

"Yes, yes, Sonia is blond! Can you see her? What's she doing?"

"I can't be a hundred percent... hmmm. It looks like she's digging around inside something. A kind of coil. Uh-huh. Yeah, she's trying to untangle something."

"That's Billy's tube!"

"OK." Clara sounded almost bored.

"What else? Where is she doing this?"

"It looks like they're near some little snack bar."

"Impossible! No way! There isn't a single touristy thing at these falls, not even a porta john. Look harder, Clara. Please."

"Sorry."

"What do you mean, sorry? She may have jumped into the falls and dragged Billy in with her!"

Clara laughed. "That woman loves herself way too much to do any bodily harm."

"Then you don't see Sonia and Billy in the water?"

"Nope."

Russell looked out across the falls. He scratched his head. It felt damp, also gummy, like thick goo stuck on his scalp. He hadn't had dandruff since The Gulf. The VA doc told him dandruff was caused by stress.

"Clara are you one hundred percent positive you don't see them floating around?"

She let out a long sigh. "See, this is where it gets annoying. I tell you they're not in the water and you still go on with it. On and on and on. No wonder your life is a mess. You have no faith, Russell. No faith in anything."

She was right. He had no faith. If pushed, he couldn't name a single thing he had faith in. "Well what should I do?"

"Wait. Wait and they'll come back."

"Soon?"

"I guess soon. I'm not that good with timetables. I told a guy his daughter would be an actress at twenty, and she's still waiting for her big break."

"How old is she now?"
"Russell go back to the car."
"Can you see me out here, Clara? Can you actually see these falls?"
"No, but I can hear them, they're loud. Now goodbye."
"Goodbye, Clara," he said into the roar.

CHAPTER 74

Soon

Russell had begun to think of himself as a homing pigeon, in that once again he was back in the car. He told Peaches and Tad, "They'll be here soon."

The girl leaned forward putting her arms around his neck. "You've seen them? Billy and Sonia?"

"Not exactly." He kind of unraveled her.

"How do you know they're coming back?"

"Yeah, dude, explain that, would you?"

"Faith," said Russell. "Meanwhile I think we should put on a little country western in honor of Billy, and to help pass the time."

"No country western." Tad was rapping his knuckles on the window. "It's bad enough we have to listen to that crap with Billy here but now that Billy's gone..."

Pivoting in the seat Russell lunged. It hurt when his stomach slammed the seat, but the look on Tad's face was worth it. "Take it back."

"I take it back," the kid whimpered.

"He's sorry!" Once again Peaches to his rescue.

Does nothing in this world ever change? Russell convinced he wouldn't take a clear breath till he saw Billy shuffling toward the car. Despite what Clara said about everything being OK. She was right. He had no faith.

After too many country western songs a thump on the trunk startled them all. Sonia's face appearing at Russell's side window. His jaw dropped then he jumped out of the car. She was alone. He looked around the area. "Where's Billy?"

"He'll be here soon."

That *soon* again. If he were the paranoid type, he'd swear these women were all in the same secret worldwide club with its own secret lingo.

"Where is Billy, where have you been all this time? I was about to call the cops." That part was a lie, the last thing he wanted was police intervention. Nina probably has him registered as a car thief in all 52 states.

"Billy is fine. The Ranger's bringing him in his truck."

"What Ranger, what truck? Why can't he walk on his own? You did! What's going on, Sonia?"

She leaned against the car crossing one ankle over the other, looking bright, flushed, animated. Sexy. No – sexual. Sonia (and he should know) looked like she just had great sex.

"Sonia you didn't... not with Billy?"

"What?"

"Well you're flushed."

"You mean sex?"

"Well, yeah."

"Did you flip your trip?"

"It's just that you seem, so, well, perky." He sounded like a wimp; he knew it; yet he still held out a little hope she might return. "I mean with Billy missing, both of you, for so long. Well naturally one would expect the worst."

"*One* would." Her voice dripped sarcasm.

"What's going on?" Tad yelled out the window. "Did you try and *off yourself*, Sonia?"

She laughed throwing her head back, the long, shiny white neck gleaming against her green ski jacket. It is a beautiful neck, thought Russell, coughing spasmodically.

"I hear some lung congestion," she said.

"Well, Nurse Sonia, you should know." And he was pissed all over again, knew she'd never fuck him; she was done. Russell put on his *Gulf face*: the hardest, meanest, most cruel expression he could muster.

"I guess they told you," she said.

"Who cares what you are? I want to know why Billy is coming back with a fucking Ranger?"

"It's no big deal." She began fussing with her braid, pulling off the tie-thingy at the end, shaking her hair loose. It hung limp rather than sexy which had probably been her intention; toy with him while she stalled.

"Tie it back up," he barked. "You look old with it down."

"That was unnecessarily nasty."

"I can be a real bastard."

"So I gather."

"I'm still waiting to see Billy. If anything's happened to him you're going to find yourself in deep shit Sonia."

Peaches got out of the car, then, the two of them hugging.

"She wouldn't let anything happen to Billy, right Sonia? Tell him."

But Sonia kept quiet, a smile he saw as mercenary moving across her face. Obviously she was enjoying his torment. He wondered if she tormented Edward when she lived with him; deciding the answer was yes. A definite yes.

"If he doesn't get here in the next five minutes, totally unharmed, I'm turning you in."

"Honestly Russell."

Tad had gotten out, too. Looking worried, scratching his belly under his shirt and saying, "What will you charge Sonia with?"

Russell clenched his toes. The sky kept changing – one minute light-gray turning to nearly black, as clouds rolled in like thunderheads, or an ominous sea. The sky over the falls – wild and unpredictable. Like these kids.

What could he charge her with?

CHAPTER 75

Sonia darlin'

Tad was writing on the hood of the car. In the dirt and dust and filth and residue from all the states they'd passed through all these weeks. A few times Russell thought of getting it washed but then it would start to snow again.

I LOVE BILLY stretched big across the hood. Before Russell could comment, a Jeep painted school bus yellow came zipping toward them.

"It's Billy!" yelled Tad. "See that's his arm waving out the window!"

Sure enough, a camel-coated arm could be seen flapping out the Jeep window. The driver tooting the horn a few times, short and cheery, seemed to announce *all is well*. Peaches and Tad were yelling and jumping up and down. Sonia just kept smiling in that enigmatic way.

Wipe it off, Russell wanted to say. He wanted to shake her silly. He wanted to throw her to the ground and jump her.

Aided by the Ranger, the old man was climbing out of the Jeep. "Come and get him!" the Ranger called. A stocky man in a tan uniform that reminded Russell of the army. Billy stood holding onto the Ranger's arm.

"Where's his walker?" Russell looked pointedly at Sonia. "Why can't he use the walker?"

"It's gone."

"Come again?"

"He doesn't need it, he can walk on his own."

"Have you... he can't take two steps without that walker. Have you fucking lost your mind? Where is it?"

Tad began pacing in circles.

Sonia raised her chin looking him square in the eyes. "I tried him out on the path. I tested him, he did great. We walked around a lot, we talked. Billy doesn't need it."

"This man is still waiting," the Ranger called out.

Russell grabbed her by the shoulders. "If he doesn't need it, then why isn't he sprinting over to us? Huh? Huh?" He shook her a little.

"Get off me!" Sonia shoved him.

"Why isn't Billy trotting over? I'll tell you why! Because you're full of shit, Sonia, that's why!" He was screaming in her face but didn't care.

"I said let go of me!"

"Hey, let the little lady go!" the Ranger shouted.

"I should throw you over the falls, Sonia. That's what I should do."

He held her by the shoulders. A look crossed her face. He couldn't tell exactly what. Shame, maybe? Fear? Neither. Sonia, he realized, was incapable of feeling much of anything.

"One last chance. Tell me where his walker is."

With her face and tone perfectly blank she said, "Over the falls."

A gasp out of Peaches, or Tad, or both.

Russell let her go. He bent bracing his hands against his knees. There's nothing left to happen, he thought staring at the ground. It's all been done.

"Sir!" the Ranger called out, "one of you has to come and get this man."

"Go," was all he said to her.

"Hey, nobody bosses me around."

"Go get Billy or I'll leave you here to die in the desert." Russell heard a soldier say it to another soldier. It was *Jones* rather than Billy.

"Desert?" Tad was springing from the eyes, all bobble-headed.

Peaches in her begging voice, "Sonia, you better do it."

Cursing under her breath, swinging those long arms, she strode toward Billy.

The old man calling out, "Sonia darlin'."

CHAPTER 76

Nowhere Particular

She could hardly hold Billy up. Russell stood by watching her struggle. He almost laughed. He knew that feeling: Billy's weight against you like a sack of rocks. Now Sonia would know, too, every day. Sonia would know Billy and his body on a more intimate level.

"Sir, I think you're being unfair on the little lady."

He ignored the Ranger. The old man could hardly take a step on his own, Sonia practically dragging him, instructing him to lift one foot then the other, which Billy didn't seem able to do.

"The little lady here is doing her best, you two men should be helping her."

Go eat some tree bark, thought Russell. He knew those *Ranger types*. Cushy job, new Jeep paid for by the government, decent salary and benefits. Without the uniform, the guy was a paunchy nothing.

Sonia, struggling under the old man, eventually made it to the car. "I'm born again," Billy was saying. "That's how I can walk, with the help of God."

Russell waited outside the car, till the kids had the old man settled, before he got behind the wheel. When Sonia started to slide in next to him, he jerked a thumb. "You in the back. He's your charge now."

"My *charge*?" Sonia went livid. "What the hell is this, Charles Dickens?" She slammed the car door. Leo's door.

"You break that door you pay for it," Russell shouted. "Out of your nurse salary."

"I'll pay!" said Billy. "I pay for what my kids break."

Russell ordered Tad to sit up front. He had enough of the girls. Even Tad was better, at least weirdly predictable. The girls were beyond the realm.

"Say goodbye to the falls," he told them. "Especially Billy's walker." Floating downstream somewhere. Where Russell wished he was floating. Alone. On a quiet river. Under a summer sun. In a black inner-tube with his legs dangling, and nowhere in particular he had to be.

CHAPTER 77

United Front

Now it was hard on Sonia all the time. Russell didn't give a shit. The kids talked about getting Billy another *amazing Technicolor walker* which Russell vetoed. *Absolute power* he thought, getting off on those two words. Almost better than sex.

Laughing to himself, he watched Sonia struggle getting the old man in and out of the car, in and out of diners, motels, even the shower. Billy without his walker was a major problem. Sonia's. As long as she stayed. She gave up the showers, saying she had to stand inside with him, switching to baths. Nurse or no nurse, Russell could tell this bothered her. Billy, of course, turning it into a sexual farce.

"She washes me *everywhere*," he bragged at breakfast.

"Sonia's a nurse, she's used to it," said Tad. "See how I spread the butter right to the edges of the toast."

Sonia banged her fist on the table. "He washes his own ass, he's not armless. That's where I draw the line."

"I'm harmless," said Billy.

"What if he has a stroke and he can't move?" Peaches wanted to know. "Then what will you do, Sonia?"

"She'll wash his ass," said Russell.

Nothing else had changed yet he felt cheerful, almost gleeful, observing Sonia handle Billy. He felt tons lighter with the old man around Sonia's neck now.

"She'll have to wipe it if he has a stroke," Tad was saying.

"We already covered that." Sonia's blue eyes smoldered. She turned to Russell. "You know, you're actually worse than Edward." Maggie's hatred turning pale by comparison.

After a few more days of hard labor Sonia tried cornering him. He'd left the motel dining room before the rest had finished dinner. His meal stank: dried out meatloaf, over-salted mashed potatoes, mushy green beans. Wonder Bread and packets of margarine. Tad put a slice on his head.

Sonia must've planned on following him, coming up from behind as he was getting ready to put his room card in the door. "Look, I may have misjudged Billy's condition. But I swear to you, after we said the prayers at the falls, he started walking around as normal as you and I. I swear to you."

Rot in hell, thought Russell. It was breaking her, all the lifting and dragging. She looked weakened. "You're a nurse, what's the problem?"

"I'm a nurse, not a male orderly! I'm going to have a permanent back problem if this goes on much longer."

"Poor you." He chuckled inserting the card. "You can always leave, bail out and go home." To Edward. He sneaked a look at her nipples through the white T-shirt. Showing on purpose, he would bet money. During dinner she wore a black V-neck sweater on top. Nipples that he'd never know up close again. It didn't matter. He wanted to be rid of her. All of them. The kids might have their differences but they were a united front. Russell was the enemy. He'd break them till they begged to leave. He wasn't quite sure exactly how. Not yet. Then he'd buy Billy a new walker and finish the trip in peace.

He opened the room door, went inside and shut it in her face. Sitting on the bed he phoned Stan.

CHAPTER 78

In the Room

Stan you better pick up, he was thinking.

"I thought for sure you fell in the falls," said his brother after they said *hello.*

"You should only know."

"What's that supposed to mean?"

"I'm too tired to go into it. Someday I'll tell you. Not now."

"Bro, you've got my curiosity *riled*. By the way, I hate to say this, but the rest of your fish died."

"All the guppies are dead???"

"I did exactly what you told me but they started dying, almost one by one. It was crazy. I'd come in to feed them and I'd see this little guy floating at the top, then the next time another one belly-up."

"Did you scoop out the dead one each time?"

"What do you think? Of course I did! In case there was some fish virus going around. Some kind of gill plague."

"Stan, why didn't you tell me this earlier? When it first started? I might have come up with an idea. Or told you to call a vet."

"You're practically having a nervous breakdown. I haven't heard you this bad since you fell off that truck and they sent you home from The Gulf. I wasn't about to burden you with the fish. What do you take me for, some insensitive guy?"

CHAPTER 79

Greenland

So his guppies were all dead. It figures. He lowered himself into a brown vinyl chair. The kind that squeaks. A small rip where you'd rest your head back. He kept clear of the rip that showed some yellow stuffing. His fish were dead, his barometer stuck on *SNOW*. Even during summer.

"Interesting," said Russell.

"What's interesting?" said Stan.

He was thinking if he lived in Greenland it would be a correct barometric reading. He didn't live in Greenland. Right now he'd give anything to see a green lawn, a green pasture. Smell some spring, feel the gentle breezes. He was a lot more tired than he'd realized. And despite what he knew about cheap motels Russell let his head drift back till it rested on the rip.

"Stan, I'm beat."

"I can hear it in your voice. I heard it in your first sentence."

"Have you seen anymore of Nina?"

"Why do you ask?"

"I've been ducking her for weeks, you know that. She's probably psychotic at this point. Every time I see a cop car I expect to be pulled over." He let his eyes close. "It's not easy on me, Stan."

"Nina isn't that bad."

Russell felt all his molecules go on red alert. His eyes popped open and he leaned forward in the chair. "What are you talking about? Not so bad? To turn me in, not so bad? Or not so bad as a woman? A girlfriend, maybe? What's going on?"

"I have been seeing her, somewhat."

"You said she's ugly!"

"That doesn't mean we can't go out."

"I thought you only went for pretty women, like Clara?"

"That one's too crazy. Besides, I think she's saving herself for you."

Clara, for him? She sounded like she was about to vomit whenever they spoke. At his house, for instance, she acted downright unfriendly, actually becoming hostile about the squirrel. Like she was the one it attacked! Black squirrels, she'd said. It was ridiculous. Halfway across the country and he hasn't seen one freakin' black squirrel.

"I think you're mistaken about Clara."

He wasn't an idiot; Stan trying to soften him up on account of screwing Nina regularly now. He was sure of it. "I feel totally betrayed."

"Bro, I can't help myself."

"There's women all over the place! At the plant! What about all those hot women who work at the plant, why can't you get involved with them? Why does it have to be Nina?" And, Leo, he thought. Russell picturing a blunt object coming down hard on his skull.

"I don't know, I don't know. That mean little face of hers, it just gets to me." Stan sounded genuinely perplexed.

We're all lost, thought Russell, hanging up without saying goodbye.

CHAPTER 80

Plenty of Room for Horses

When he came down in the morning, Tad and Peaches were alone at the table. They looked glum. Though it held their usual large spread of egg dishes, hash browns, breakfast sausage, plus a basket of muffins and assorted jams in mini-pots. Peaches seemed listless as she picked at her *western* scraping off some of the red sauce.

Russell sat down without speaking. He studied the muffins in the basket. It hadn't snowed during the night, and sunlight blasted through the smudged picture window. *I hate this room, it's drab*, Sonia said last night when it was a dining room. Now she hates everything, he thought. Especially me.

"We'll make tracks today, if Sonia and Billy get their act together before noon."

Peaches sighed still picking at the omelette. "Don't count on that."

"What's going on?"

Tad belched. "Sonia's out. I heard her on the phone with the airlines last night. Then she talked to Ed."

Ed? Edward! The husband. "She's leaving us?" Russell could feel the grin spreading across his face. "What about you two?"

"We haven't made up our mind." Tad dumping all the muffins onto the table then twirling the wicker basket under his finger. "I'm practicing magic, watch me make the muffins jump back in the basket."

Ignoring the bullshit Russell said, "I thought you three were a team?"

"We are and we aren't," said Peaches. "Sonia has a future. A career. Plus Edward would take her back. What do we have? Besides, I really wanted to see the ranch. Billy has a special horse waiting for me. A white stallion." She looked wistful.

Russell almost feeling sorry for the beautiful screwed up

girl with the wild hair. She, both these kids, honestly believed the ranch existed. The life Billy had painted so colorfully. Easy enough to believe – what with the dull unchanging landscape and mostly gray skies. "There's no ranch, it's just a white house on a cul de sac," Russell said. "Tad put the muffins back."

They both looked blank. Peaches finally saying, "What about the horses?"

"No horses. No ranch. It's all in Billy's imagination."

"Have you *been there*, dude? Seen for yourself?" The kid was looking unhinged.

"No, but Billy told me..."

"Then you don't *know*, you don't know nothin'."

"Look. Billy specifically told me it was a white house on a cul de sac. Its own cul de sac, if that makes a difference," Russell added.

"See! You screwed up that part, dude! It's on its own cul de sac which means there's plenty of room for horses."

Peaches brightened. "That's true! I could still have my horse."

"Pass the muffins, please?"

Tad chucked them back in the basket handing it over to Russell. He took one and bit in. Cranberry? He thought he'd taken corn but the berries must be hidden deep inside. Preoccupied with the current situation, he hadn't noticed the berries. It was surprisingly juicy, fresh and delicious. He took another bite.

The kids sat watching him.

"You can wish till the cows come home. There's no horses. You should both seriously think about hooking a ride with Sonia. I'm sure Edward will be happy to pay for your plane tickets, too." Russell laughed peeling the muffin paper all the way down. The next bite was full of cranberries.

Tad screwed up his face. Russell ignored him enjoying the muffin. This morning he felt more relaxed than – how long? A decade, maybe; maybe longer.

"This would be even more delicious with that apple butter. Peaches could you pass me some?"

"Here." Sounding pissed she pushed the little jar toward him. He noticed she looked messy. Not just the wild hair – that was her normal. She looked unkempt though he couldn't say why. Something about her eyes. Both kids seemed ready to orbit. Great, thought Russell. Godspeed. Like the army said when they sent you off to die.

He should probably go find Billy. Sonia may have taken off

in secret; she was capable. Didn't she screw him without using a rubber? After that knife wound guy bled all over her. What a bitch. He pushed his chair back. "I'm going to get Billy."

Neither of the kids said anything. They seemed to have already vacated. If not physically, at least in spirit.

CHAPTER 81

Unlocked

Billy's door wasn't fully shut. No Billy in the room. He called out, then he looked in the bathroom, then inside the closet where he instructed the old man to keep his suitcase. Suitcase still in there. He looked under the bed. Filthy. Lots of dust and some dead roaches. He ignored his phone vibrating against his chest.

Russell went to the kids' room which they never bothered to lock. It didn't matter to them what might be stolen since they'd paid for practically nothing. He couldn't get a handle on whether Sonia's things were gone, since hers and Peaches' were hopelessly mixed together.

Did Billy leave with Sonia? Unlikely. It was the sixty-four-thousand dollar question that Russell wasn't prepared to answer.

He stood out in the hall. People coming and going. I just need Billy alive and well, he was thinking. Then he never wanted to lay eyes on the old man again, hear his stinking songs, or remember a single story about Shelley Lee.

CHAPTER 82

Beyond the Earth

Nina picked up. At least he assumed it was her voice, he couldn't actually remember, it felt like another lifetime.

"Nina?"

"Yeah?"

"It's Russell."

"Russell!"

She didn't even sound pissed but more like she'd connected with the dead. "Is it really *you*?" This only adding to his sense of being beyond the earth.

"It's really me."

"You fucking son of a bitch! When I see you I'm gonna tear you a new asshole."

In half a second she'd gotten her circuits restored and was tearing him a new asshole. "I know, I know, I've got a lot of explaining to do."

"You missed the wedding."

He wasn't sure he heard correctly. "Did someone we both know get married?"

She honked out a laugh. "I married your big galupe of a brother. I never thought I could love again."

"No kidding." No kidding for sure. Nice of Stan to let him know. Then thinking *Why stare a gift horse in the face* (even one with a horse face)? "That's great, Nina, congratulations."

He was picturing all the little *scrunched-face Ninas*, the *little Stans*, his nieces and nephews to be, when she said, "How is Billy Bud Wilcox doing?"

Russell clutched his chest. A young couple, practically humping down the hall, stopped their gyrations to squeeze past him. "Are you OK mister?" the girl said.

"Billy Bud Wilcox is doing great." He leaned against the wall for support.

"Hurry on home so we can all be a family." Nina sounding so happy it was almost inconceivable. "By the way, Leo says if you got any scratches on the car, not to worry, they can always be compounded out."

He shook his head, blinking.

"Russell, are you there?"

"You're fading, Nina."

Down the long dreary hallway he watched the young couple, the guy's hand turning on the girl's ass like winding a clock. He wondered why Stan hadn't phoned him with the news but already had the answer. The whole thing was falling apart. Russell didn't even own a guppy he could call his own.

CHAPTER 83

Shave and a Haircut

"Whatcha doin'?" He turned to find Billy riding on the back of a huge guy he recognized as the suitcase porter from the front door. "Say hello to Ike," the old man chimed. "Like Ike and Tina Turner, but this feller swears he can't sing a note."

"I can't." Ike puffing under Billy's weight. "Can I put you down here?"

"Put him down," said Russell. "Where's Sonia?"

Billy slid down Ike's back, more or less landing on his feet. "Shave and a haircut," said the old man wobbling and grinning.

"Where is Sonia?"

"She split!"

"She took off and left you alone?"

"Nope. First she got Ike, then she split."

"That bitch."

"Stop yer cussin'! Sonia had to go, Edward couldn't wait any more. He waited all this time for his Sonia darlin', and finally when he couldn't take another second of it, she realized. She came to the *re-a-liz-ation*."

"Yeah, that sounds just like her."

"The fly hit the wall." Billy's voice had gone soft. "Not like my Shelley Lee." He wagged his head. "She never came to the *re-a-liz-ation*."

Ike kept turning from Billy to Russell like watching a tennis match. "He paid me to stay with him," said Ike, "but I need to get back on the door."

"You got ants in your pants?" said the old man.

"Sure, Ike, you go ahead, I've got him covered." Russell could only imagine how much cash had crossed Ike's palm. "Where is your suitcase?" he asked Billy.

"I locked it in the bag room," said Ike.

"Good. OK. Well, then. Billy, are you ready to roll?"

"I'm ready to rock n roll!"

Russell slung his arm under the old man's. "Sonia snuck off like a rat."

"She said goodbye to me," said Ike.

"She gave me a tongue kiss," said Billy.

CHAPTER 84

Including the Stems

The lobby area was a mess of bags, everyone checking out at the same time.

"Those are all my bags," Peaches was saying. "Sonia took hers."

He stared at the girl. "If you knew Sonia took her stuff then you had to know she was leaving."

Peaches twisted a lock of hair. "Well sort of."

"It's complex, dude! Sonia is a complex person." Tad twitching like a jumping bean. Russell naturally assumed he was high.

"Oh forget it!" He blew them off with a wave of his arm. And forget Sonia ever existed. The same went for Stan. Once he got home, unloaded the car back on Leo, that would be that. He never wanted to see his brother again.

"You two at least help Billy get in the car."

❧

The next morning Peaches and Tad did not come to breakfast. When Russell knocked on their door then pushed it open it was empty. *Fled* popped in his mind. He next went in search of the suitcase. Though it was still in Billy's room, the bundles of bills in large denominations, stacked neatly and wrapped in their paper bank bands, had been torn apart, cash scattered in the suitcase like used tissues.

In the lobby Russell said, "We probably should count the money and see how much you've got left." The old man began to cry over what he called *the disappearance of my Shelley Lee.*

"It won't be the same now." He sobbed, his cheeks and forehead unusually blotchy. People were turning around and looking at them; at Russell; as if he'd done something to harm the old man.

"Billy, listen to me. Listen."

BBW covered his ears. "It won't be the same ever again." He continued to sob.

At the door Ike called out a cheery *good journey*. Billy ignoring it. Another fifteen minutes passed getting him out of the building, across the motel gravel area and settled in the car.

With Billy up front, next to him, for the first time, they crossed the Iowa state line. Roadside, a wooden sign: WELCOME TO NEBRASKA.

"Hey, Billy, welcome to Nebraska!"

The old man was despondent. "Will ya look at all this empty space," he kept saying. "Just look at it."

"Nebraska is a pretty wide open state. I thought you liked the open plains, the wide open ranges?" Russell was fumbling for the right words. "Like the ranch." Throw him a bone – what's the harm?

The ranch. That carrot BBW waved at the kids for hundreds and hundreds and hundreds of miles. Till an unruly rabbit named Sonia crept from her rabbit hole devouring what she could. Including the stems.

"Not Nebraska!" Billy shrieked.

Confused, and tired, for a moment Russell thought he'd gone the wrong direction. That can't be, he thought, saying, "Excuse me?"

The old man was crying again, slapping the seat, and nothing Russell said or offered could calm him down. "All this empty space," he kept moaning.

"We'll come to a town soon, a city. How'd you like to visit Lincoln, Nebraska?"

BBW cried harder.

"Wouldn't that be fun? We'll spend a day in Lincoln and you can take in the sights. How'd you like that? Then it won't feel so empty."

So far in terms of driving Nebraska had been a pleasure. Bright sun and deep blue sky, the long straight roads with little traffic, and no kids in the car. No kids! The idea of detouring off the route into a city wasn't his first choice, but Billy's drawn out misery was becoming relentless. One worry leaves, another begins. Does life have to be like this? He remembered the docu-drama of the woman in white following her bliss. "Where is my bliss?" said Russell.

Billy was sniffling and blowing, tissue after tissue. "My kids are gone. My Shelley Lee. It's all empty inside." He hung his head for several miles.

I know what you mean, Russell wanted to say but knew it

wouldn't get through to him. The old man was done with flashes of false hope. The future didn't hold much for him to get excited about, and Billy wasn't stupid.

"Let me ask you something, Billy. You had all those wives, yet you never had any children?"

He sniffled and blew his nose again. "Nine."

"You have nine kids?"

"Had. No more."

They drove behind a horse trailer, the wide rumps sticking out the back, horse tails swishing in the open air. Sonia and Peaches crossed his mind. No shame, those two. Sashayed around naked – soft mounds of pubic hair like tiny pillows. Somewhere to lay your head, he thought. Feeling extra horny now that they wouldn't be coming back.

"Gossip," the old man was saying. "Plain ole gossip. Folks say I abandoned my kids but you know what? They abandoned me. That's right. I give 'em everything I had to give. They grew up and never came back. They don't even show up at Shelley Lee's wake. Imagine that."

He was *tsk tsking* but at least with some energy. He'd shaken off his sad mood and now he was angry.

For a while Russell played tag with the horse trailer, passing it by, slowing down, and vice-versa.

"Those nags are nothin'," said Billy. "I've got horses will blow your eyeballs out of their sockets."

"How can you judge a horse when you can only see its behind?" Peaches crossed his mind – now there was a great rump.

"I can! I'm a first rate judge of livestock. You wait and see. I might even let you ride the white stallion."

Ah, jeez, we're back to that, thought Russell.

CHAPTER 85

Seat Belts

The horse trailer finally made a turn off and Billy wanted to go after it. "Let's follow that van and make a deal," he said. "I might want to buy one of them horses."

"You said those horses stank, you called them nags, I'm not following the horse trailer, it's off our route."

"See! The route again, always the route. That's why I get mopey in this car, I can't stand keepin' to the route. I like the open road. Free, like a little birdie."

Talk about delusional, thought Russell. All of a sudden he'd kill for a cigarette. At a shack along the road he pulled over. He told Billy to wait, he'd be right out.

"Maybe you want a candy bar or something?"

The old man didn't answer. I'll get him a few packs of M&M's, thought Russell; the old man's favorites being the yellows and greens.

Inside the shack was another of those glass cases holding the usual assortment of beaded junk, belts, tobacco pouches, boxes of cigarettes. Sonia or Peaches – he couldn't remember which – kept on about a turquoise hair clip. It would have looked good on either girl. Pretty on the blond, exotic in the black hair. He tapped the case asking the blubbery guy, "Is that one a hair clip?"

"That's dope paraphernalia." Staring into space the guy looked bored. "You lookin' to get some Fred?"

"Fred? That's not my name. You got me confused with someone else."

The guy grinned crookedly. "You smoke-em Fred." The stupid jerk was laughing at him.

Russell felt embarrassed. Tad was right, he was definitely not cool. Didn't even know the latest in dope lingo or dope paraphernalia. Even the latest dope.

In his day you smoked pot, graduating to peyote, and the really crazy people took acid. Tad and the girls, they know it all. An ugly hick like this guy making him feel stupid. Russell clenched his toes. "Give me a pack of Camels."

He paid. Staring into his palm at the small amount of change. Cigarettes had gotten expensive during the time he'd given up smoking. "Do you have M&M's?"

"Just what's in the case." The guy turned away to wait on another customer.

"Hold it. Give me those Baby Ruths. Three."

The guy was about to get involved with that other redneck who just walked in, a rag-head who called him by name and looked jumpy. These country chats... they could go on for an hour or longer. Russell wanted his cigarettes and candy and to get the hell out of there.

❧

Next to Leo's car, a girl with a big shaggy dog was chatting up Billy through the open window. Wait a second, thought Russell. Did that make Leo *his* brother-in-law? Freaky.

The girl turned and looked at him. Billy practically hanging out the window. "How did you get the window down?" he asked the old man.

"It was down."

"Nope."

"Yep. You didn't notice. You was busy lookin' at them horse rumps, I saw ya."

One girl, and he trucks out the hillybilly charm. This one looked all of sixteen. If. Billy telling her about the ranch. The girl was skinny and strung out, but the old man smiled adoringly saying, "Katrina darlin'."

Russell sprinted around the car jumping into the driver seat. He gave a few toots then peeled away, chunks of gravel hitting the sides of Leo's paint job.

"You're a drag," said Billy. "She's so cute. That Katrina. I could have fun with her. She looks just like Shelley Lee looked before..." he started to sniffle.

God, thought Russell, the guy is unstoppable. Yeah go ahead and make her your ninth or tenth wife.

"Forget it, Billy, she's out of your league. You can do heaps better." Heaps better? He never used that expression. He tossed a Baby Ruth into Billy's lap. Russell thinking they'd have to find a one-hour dry cleaner and get that camel hair coat fumigated.

"Baby Ruth. I like Baby Ruth." Finally the old man was smiling.

Russell noticed he was having some trouble peeling the wrapper. "Here, let me," he said. Tearing an opening with his teeth and handing it back to Billy. "Umm. Chocolate smells good."

"Ya think so? I want to smell pussy. Let's go to a cat house." He dropped his candy bar rubbing his veined hands together. "I want them cats crawlin' all over me. Lickin' and purrin'. Lickin' and purrin'."

Yeah, thought Russell. That instinct must stay with you a long time, long after your parts have worn out. A sobering thought.

❧

What also stayed with them was the crystal clear sky, and snowcapped mountains in the distance. Billy claimed to have seen a family of hawks. Russell was doubtful, saying he understood hawks to be loners.

"Hawks ain't lonely."

"I said loner, not lonely."

"It's the same." The old man took off his seat belt.

"Hey! Put the belt back on, nobody in this car without their belt on."

Billy shook his head stubbornly. "Peaches didn't wear her belt."

"Of course she did."

"She took it off to give me blow jobs."

Russell jerked the wheel and the car zig-zagged. Billy started to giggle. "She gave it nice and low on the shaft."

"I was in this car everyday, don't you think I'd know if Peaches was giving you a blow job?"

"Don't know what ya know."

"If you think you're messing with my head, well you're not."

The old man still refusing to put the belt on.

"OK. Leave it off. If we get into an accident they'll ticket me and add points to my license. Possibly put me in jail. Who will you get to drive you to the ranch?" Who could put up with you?

"One of your jailers," said Billy. "Those prison guards just love country western, they'll drive me to the ranch. Then I won't have to put up with your bullshit no more."

"I guess you should know about prison guards, having been *inside.*" If that story Billy told was even true. "So you think I've been bad to you, huh?"

"Not to me, to my kids."

"Billy, you've got to clock into reality. Those three... they were not your kids, those three were..." It was useless. Truth being the one thing Billy didn't hold in surplus.

"Look, if we can find a cat house I'll take you."

The old man grinned. "That's the ticket!"

"First we have to get you cleaned up. Get the coat cleaned, and a shave and bath and a haircut."

"Sonia gave a good bath, she's a nurse. Nurses and airline stewardesses, if what you're lookin' for is good clean screwin'."

Russell groaned, passing a pickup with migrant workers and farm equipment crammed together in the open back section. He wondered if the workers were cold? The men looked from somewhere south of the border, the winter had to be rough on them.

"Those guys must be freezing."

"Down Mexico way," Billy sang out.

CHAPTER 86

Federal Style

"You talk persnickety," said the old man.

Russell wished for another horse trailer so they could switch the conversation back to horse rumps. Peaches and the blow jobs in the car had caused him some anxiety.

After another hour or so of driving, around four, they stopped for the night at a Victorian B&B painted yellow. The Sunshine Inn. "Is this our cat house?" Billy wanted to know.

"This is where we sleep for the night. I hope. Pretty nice, wouldn't you say?" He sat there a moment taking it all in. The big Victorian had one of those rounded turrets and a lot of white gingerbread trim along the porch. Under a dousing of snow, thick green shrubbery poked up around the foundation. Someone had shoveled the brick front walkway.

"Isn't this quaint and lovely," said Russell.

"How'd you find this place?"

"Someone mentioned it in some state. Said if we got this far we should stay here. I wrote it down."

"Well ain't you organized."

Russell got out of the car. He stood on the sidewalk looking at the house. Lovely, he thought again. Lovely being a word he usually reserved for a certain type of woman who was very pretty but also feminine and soft. And, rare these days. One time he'd called Sonia lovely; quickly realizing his mistake.

A softness coming off the house seemed to enter him and pass through, like a wandering ghost from a faraway time. He needed to be closer, taking a few steps from the car.

"I want out!" Billy was shouting.

He let the old guy have his fit then finally helped him out. Now that the kids were gone he had to buy Billy a new walker.

"Look," said the old man pointing up. "A man sittin' on that roof!"

Across the street from the yellow B&B, a man was on the roof of another house, large and square, with a flat roof. Russell believed it was called the Federal Style. He didn't know from dope but he knew a little about houses – thanks to Maggie and her compulsive decorating schemes. Up there, the seated man wore a red plaid jacket with his legs dangling over. He seemed to be relaxing. Though maybe a bit dangerously. But what isn't dangerous? Wasn't he out taking a walk on a nice sunny day, like this one, when a squirrel came from nowhere (well out of that tree) and jumped down and bit him. Danger hovered. Russell believed that. From everywhere and nowhere.

I'm nowhere, he thought. Finding this strangely exhilarating. Maybe it was the same for the guy on the roof. He and Billy continued to watch.

A sneeze. A wind gust. Even a *family of hawks* (Billy's notion) flying past squawking and distracting the guy; a sudden unexpected tumble toward death. Was it? Unexpected?

CHAPTER 87

Sorry

No space at The Sunshine Inn. A softly rounded, sweet voiced, pleasant looking woman about Russell's age suggested they try a place down the road called Blueberry House. Adding she was *terribly sorry*. "It's very nice, too, it's painted blue like blueberries. She made a little laugh like a swoosh of feet on a sandy beach.

Billy, over by the window, was angry and fuming, demanded to stay here, saying he wanted to *keep tabs on the guy on the roof*. "Can I see the guy from that blueberry place?"

"He means the man sitting on the roof across the street."

"Oh, he's just a roofer doing some repairs."

"Can I see him?" The old man sounding shrill.

"Billy I don't think so."

"Then I ain't goin'. Tell her that's that."

Russell approached him, attempting to move him toward the door, but BBW had stiffened his body. "C'mon, Billy, let's go check out the Blueberry House."

"Hate 'em, won't touch 'em."

"Blueberries?" The woman was smiling. "Everyone loves blueberries. They're good for you."

"They got maggots."

"Excuse me?"

Russell pulled on his arm. "C'mon."

"They got maggots. Soak 'em in water and watch those maggots rise to the top of the bowl."

He was losing patience but didn't want to act rude in front of this woman. "OK, then we'll skip the blueberries but we're staying there if they have room."

Billy jutted out his whiskery white beard. An affectation he took on after the kids vanished. "Nope and nope."

"Sir..."

"You shut up!"

Russell saw a look pass over her face. "Ma'am, you'll have to excuse him, he's not himself today." Or any other day. He glared at Billy wondering why he bothered. Chuck him into a Motel 6 and call it a night.

Her face, sweet in its way, looked sympathetic. He decided it was her serious brown eyes.

"Don't worry, I have an elderly father," she said.

"I ain't his father. Who says I'm elderly?"

"Ma'am, this *gentleman* is Billy Bud Wilcox, the country western singer. You may have heard of him."

"'Course she's heard of me."

"And I'm Russell, I'm driving him home to Colorado." He did not say *I'm his driver.*Those were words from the past. He looked on Billy the way this woman saw him: stained and miserable. He certainly never expected to end up this way. None of us do, thought Russell. "I also happen to be his friend." Startling himself; the moment it came out of his mouth.

For once the old man didn't speak back, curse, or hurl an insult.

"I have heard you sing on the radio," said the woman. She smiled again.

"And TV," said Russell. "He's been on TV a lot."

Stiff, unyielding, BBW remained dug in. Russell could feel him putting down roots through the floorboards. He looked at his watch. "All right. Anyway, let's get going before Blueberry House sells out, too." Fame or no fame – it wasn't going to get them a room.

The woman had tilted her head back looking at the ceiling. Automatically Russell looked up too, expecting some problem. A leak. A tree about to come crashing through. At the very least.

"I might be able to squeeze you in," she said. "There's a tiny suite in the attic." She pursed her lips. "It's three flights up. Three narrow flights."

"You got an elevator?"

"I'm afraid not, Mr. Wilcox."

"Billy we can't stay here." No way was he carrying the old man up and down three narrow flights.

"Can I see the roof guy from the attic?"

"I suppose so," she said. "But he's probably finished for the day, it's almost supper time."

"I want to stay in the attic," Billy said.

I thought you wanted to go to a cat house, Russell was thinking. BBW could change like the wind. "I can't lug you up those stairs."

"I can walk. Sonia showed me how."

"Not that again!"

"First you say the little prayer, then you give up to God. You do the offerin' then God gives over his power."

Russell was tired and hungry. He'd had enough. Good old Sonia – selling Billy an old Televangelist trick: throw away your crutches and walk for the lord. "If that works so well, why am I still dragging you around?"

"You're just my back-up." The old man actually looked perky. "Like my old back-up singers. Didn't need 'em. Kept 'em around for show. Window dressin'."

Russell was tempted to call his bluff. Let him walk up those stairs. But if he took a tumble, broke bones, it would be on his neck, his conscience. His conscience already felt burdened enough though push to shove Russell couldn't say why. What did he ever do to anyone?

"Can I sit down a minute?" Russell asked the woman.

"Sure. Both of you sit yourselves down in these nice comfy chairs." She was peering at him. "Is something the matter?"

Yes, he thought. Something. Everything. All of it. Every second is the matter.

"Everything's fine," he told her.

He sank into the chair. Wanted to yell till the walls shook. Sonia crossed his mind. Just when he thought he'd seen the last of her, she flits back like a wet ghost. Why *wet*? In his mind's eye she looked wet. Maybe from the falls, where she buried Billy's walker.

"And what about you, Mr. Wilcox? Wouldn't you like to take a chair, too?"

Billy was staring down at the floor. "You got a cat house in the neighborhood?"

The woman's hand flew to her chest. "If you mean prostitutes, that's illegal."

"So's the queen's whiskers."

Russell started to laugh. He leaned back in the chair and laughed so hard his ribs hurt.

"I don't think I want you two here," said the woman crossing her arms.

"Ma'am, please..." Before he could explain, he went on another laughing jag.

"Both of you have to leave." She pointed toward the door. "It's just like they say in PEOPLE. You celebrities are not normal. Please leave right now!"

Russell got on his feet. "Ma'am, I wasn't laughing at you. I swear. You don't quite understand, nobody could unless they'd been with us. We've been on the road for weeks and weeks. I lost count. It snowed steady, it's been a three-ring circus trying to reach Colorado." His little speech had sobered him up. "I'm kind of worn out."

"The ranch," said Billy.

Russell was too fried to even address that. "Please accept my apology. Our apology. I meant no disrespect. I think I can get him up in the attic suite."

"I can't have prostitutes here."

"Never! Never! He's an old man, half the time he doesn't realize what he's saying."

Clenching her hands, the woman seemed to falter. "I don't know. Do you understand?"

"Totally!"

"Well, then. I guess there's no harm done. If you can manage the stairs."

Russell could see doubt still lingering in her eyes. "We'll manage," he said. "And, thank you. Thank you very much. We'll manage," he said again. One way or another.

"A full pancake breakfast is included," she told them.

"No blueberries," said Billy.

"That was the other place," Russell reminded him, winking at the woman as if to say: *I told you he's senile.*

CHAPTER 88

Nice

It took a while getting Billy up three flights. Not only were they narrow but over the centuries had warped, each carpeted step angled slightly different. The old man, kind of slung across Russell's back, felt heavy as a horse. Struggling he thought: I've aged twice the normal rate.

The suite turned out to be a single bedroom containing twin beds and a bureau, plus a tiny adjoining alcove in the shape of a triangle, with two compact easy chairs and a small, oval pine table.

"Nice," said Russell.

Everything smelling clean and fresh. Pastel flowered bedspreads, pink and white striped wallpaper, an ivy border trailing the sloped ceiling. A bit feminine. Yet cozy. The bathroom was miniscule. No tub. A stall with a hand-held shower nozzle.

That should be fun, Russell thought. How would the old man stand in the shower using that thing?

"Are the cats up here?" said Billy.

"I don't want you to say that anymore, you hear me? She'll throw us out on the street."

"Who? DOCTOR WHO?"

"Very funny. The lady who owns this place, that's who."

"She's sweet on you."

Christ, thought Russell, the old man sees sex everywhere.

"She's not sweet on me. Will you put that stuff out of your mind, you're driving me crazy! You wanted to stay here to see the guy on the roof, well, look at him, you have three windows. If you start with the sex stuff she'll kick us out and we'll have to go to the blueberry place." He was beginning to talk like Billy – *the blueberry place*. He was becoming an imbecile, too.

Billy grinned and stumbled against the bureau.

"You have to let me help you till we get your new walker. Watch the furniture. That could be an antique."

"It's a bunch of crap."

"I'm going down to get your suitcase. Don't do anything! Don't go out in the hall. Stay put, OK?" He eased Billy into a chair. "Look out this window or something, I'll be right back."

Russell took his time going down. Down meant he had to turn around and come back up. Not exactly high on his list. He thought about phoning Stan, automatically reaching for his cell before he remembered: Nina. He gripped the wooden banister, pausing on the first landing.

"What am I doing here?"

Discounting Sonia's wet ghost, The Sunshine Inn had been around long enough to have a few real ghosts. Not a single one answered back or crossed his face like a web.

He went the rest of the way down, got Billy's suitcase out of the trunk, plus his own bag, bringing them inside. It felt good in the lobby area, and warm, the vintage furniture covered in fabrics of greens and gold. Two built-in bookcases, a wood stove tucked in a corner. The woman had fixed it up like a very comfortable living room. Russell thought of his own living room, empty; the plastic slip covers collecting dust.

Just before he started this trip he was on the verge of redecorating. It felt like a hundred years ago. He and Stan. The kitchen. The two of them eating turkey and drinking scotch with the strutting roosters on the wallpaper. Maggie's roosters. So far as he could tell there wasn't a single rooster in The Sunshine Inn. If he saw one he might actually break down. That would not be good. The woman was letting them stay, by a thread. One false move...

In the attic suite Billy had fallen asleep in the chair. Still in the coat, he hardly ever removed it now. When he tried to get the old man to take it off and put on his pajamas, Billy reacted like a mother cat being torn from her kittens. *Shelley Lee*! *Shelley Lee*! he'd screech until Russell backed off. Even the dirty camel hair coat had become Shelley Lee.

Watching the old man sleep, he wondered if it was inevitable? When you lose everything you ever needed, and there's only the gold records and scrapbooks around to remind you that you once had a life. I don't have a gold record, thought Russell.

He decided to let Billy sleep. Go back down and have a lobby sit. Just sit.

Out the attic windows he glimpsed the Nebraska sky. Bluer than any he'd seen in quite some time. Nebraska was damned cold but the sky seemed bright as a jewel, and almost warm. It was the kind of jewel Peaches and Sonia would go on a hunt for, blue and electrifying. "Those two," he muttered leaving the room quietly.

❧

The woman who owned the place came in to the lobby as Russell was about to sit down. "Would you like to see the evening paper?" She held it out to him.

An evening paper. Back east there hadn't been two editions of a newspaper in decades. "I would, thanks." As he accepted it from her, he took note that she didn't step away. "Have you lived here a long time?" It felt good making small talk with a normal person.

"My whole life."

"That's amazing."

"Why?" she said.

"Well, most people move around. They seem to."

"Oh?" She looked as if she never thought of this before. "Have you moved around a lot?"

"Me?" Russell scratched his head. "Not really. Except for a stint in The Gulf, you know the war, I've spent most of my life, actually all of it, in New Jersey."

He'd somehow thought of himself as a person who moved around, now realized he hadn't; hardly at all. Except for the war, like he told her, and this trip – basically he'd been as stationary as a tree. Less, even. He hadn't branched out or upward or sunk any real roots – deep or shallow. Then, while hardly moving, walking slowly toward his own home, he'd allowed himself to be bitten by a squirrel. He could have knocked it away before it got its teeth in. Or the claws.

"I once got attacked by a squirrel," he told her. *Attacked* sounded less wimpy. Besides, the wound itself had always been in question.

"Were you teasing it?"

"No. It just jumped out of a tree and attacked me. It was my own fault. It could have attacked anyone that day, but it picked me."

"I don't see how that could be your fault," she said. "It sounds like you happened to be in the wrong place at the wrong time."

"True." Though he wasn't entirely certain that was the case. Not to mention he was feeling light-headed again. Like part of his skull had lifted off, to air out the section of his brain reserved for chaos. It didn't feel bad; just different.

The unpretentious lobby had a reassuring stillness. He breathed in the wood smoke. Outside the windows, daylight was almost over. Lamps on small tables, arranged here and there, had already been switched on.

She did seem to like him. Billy was right about that. And she seemed to be a nice enough person, a nice *woman*. Not gorgeous or hot, but not shabby either. He noticed the way her strawberry-blonde hair curled around her face and shoulders, and that her light skin had a sprinkling of freckles across her nose and the tops of her hands, and he noticed her arms – sturdy under a thin, rust colored cardigan. Capable arms. The kind that could knead bread dough and roll out pie crust from scratch. He wasn't used to this type of woman.

"I have to drive Billy home to Colorado," he told her. "Then I'm on my own. Free at last." He punched the air, laughing, and the woman laughed too.

They were both silent a moment. Then Russell said, "About dinner..." and the woman said, "We serve family style. It's twenty dollars per person from soup to nuts."

"Count us in," he said. "That's if it's not too late."

She grinned. "You just made the deadline."

CHAPTER 89

Dinner

He looks like crap in that filthy coat, thought Russell. "Billy let's get you out of that coat for dinner. The nice lady is serving a nice dinner." In the chair the old man continued napping. "We have to go down to dinner, I already told her. She's making extra for us." He shook Billy's leg. Shook it again. Then it occurred to him: I'm shaking a lifeless stump.

He bent and put his ear near the old man's mouth. No air. He felt the pulse in his neck and wrist then he straightened up. Just when life starts to go smoothly...

Russell collapsed into the other chair. I can't believe this, he thought. I honestly can't. What the hell were all these weeks for? All this torture? He felt like his own life had been sucked away, too. That this was a huge *life conspiracy balloon* and they'd both gotten popped. "I was really looking forward to having dinner here," he said.

CHAPTER 90

As Long As You Like

"Suppose I stop here on the way back? Spend a couple of days?"

"I think so." She said it slowly. He saw her words like flour falling from a sifter.

It was decided. Russell would drive Billy home to Colorado. The undertaker sold him a casket and tried convincing him to put the body on a plane. Russell rented a U-Haul.

"He deserves to be taken home the way he expected," Russell told the woman. "He has, that is, he had a fear of flying. That's why I was hired to drive him." It felt important to finish the job. It felt crucial.

The woman had respect in her eyes. "Come back and stay as long as you like. I'm on my own, too, but I have a boy. Gerard. He's eight. Did you see him scoot through here on his skateboard?"

Russell shook his head. He hadn't seen anyone. "I don't even know your name," he told her.

"It's Ronni. Without the e. Short for Veronica. I have a young son," she said again, pushing out her top lip with her tongue. It was obvious she was waiting for him to say something back about her boy.

"I like kids," he said. It was true. He liked *real* kids. Not those nuts Billy had adopted.

"They can be a handful," she was saying.

She should only know.

"Ronni," he said. "Short for Veronica. Both are good names." He nodded. Relieved it wasn't Shelley or Lee.

ABOUT THE AUTHOR

SUSAN TEPPER has received many awards and honors for her writings which include poetry, creative non-fiction, essays, opinion columns, book reviews and author interviews world wide. Starting in her teen years she became a trained stage actress, and also performed as a vocalist for several well known rock, folk and country music bands. Other careers have included Interior Design, Cable TV Producer, overseas tour guide, Flight Attendant for TWA, Marketing Manager for Northwest Airlines, Red Coat at United, and Sales Rep for Sabena Belgian Air. She blames it all on a wide interest range. Since being bitten by the writing bug she hasn't turned back. What Drives Men is her eighth published book. Tepper is a native New Yorker.

ACKNOWLEDGMENTS

My deepest thanks to the many people who supported this book in many different ways. For reading it in galleys and writing such terrific blurbs, I'm indebted to my friends Robert Olen Butler, Richard Peabody, Beate Sigriddaughter, James Claffey, Michael Dwayne Smith and David S. Atkinson. To those who've given their time to my body of work, their support, and most especially their friendship I wish to thank Simon Perchik, DeWitt Henry, Judith Lawrence, Eric Darton, Jamie Cat Callan, Doug Holder, Alex M. Pruteanu, Gloria Mindock, Marie Fitzpatrick, Harvey Araton, Donna Baier Stein, Alexander Neubauer, Laurie Graff, Tree Riesener, Steven V. Ramey, Digby Beaumont, W.F. Lantry, Kathleen Fitzpatrick, Sande Boritz Berger, Terry Kennedy, Dennis Mahagin, Laura Roberts, Margaret Sefton, Kari Nguyen, and so many more kind hearts. A special thanks to my dear late mother, writer Estelle Bruno, who laughed like crazy when I read her the early drafts. And, finally, to Steve Glines, with whom I've been down this road before, friends to the end.